Thomas Hardy

**The Trumpet-Major. A Tale**

Vol. 3

Thomas Hardy

**The Trumpet-Major. A Tale**
*Vol. 3*

ISBN/EAN: 9783743343764

Manufactured in Europe, USA, Canada, Australia, Japa

Cover: Foto ©Andreas Hilbeck / pixelio.de

Manufactured and distributed by brebook publishing software (www.brebook.com)

Thomas Hardy

**The Trumpet-Major. A Tale**

# CONTENTS

OF

# THE THIRD VOLUME.

## CHAPTER XXIX.

### A DISSEMBLER.

To cursory view, John Loveday seemed to accomplish this with amazing ease. Whenever he came from barracks to Overcombe, which was once or twice a week, he related news of all sorts to her and Bob with infinite zest, and made the time as happy a one as had ever been known at the mill, save for himself alone. He said nothing of Festus, except so far as to inform Anne that he had expected to see him and been disappointed. On the evening after the King's arrival at

Weymouth John appeared again, staying to supper and describing the royal entry, the many tasteful illuminations and transparencies which had been exhibited, the quantities of tallow candles burnt for that purpose, and the swarms of aristocracy who had followed the King thither.

When supper was over Bob went outside the house to shut the shutters, which had, as was often the case, been left open some time after lights were kindled within. John still sat at the table when his brother approached the window, though the others had risen and re-tired. Bob was struck by seeing through the pane how John's face had changed. Through-out the supper-time he had been talking to Anne in the gay tone habitual with him now, which gave greater strangeness to the gloom of his present appearance. He remained in thought for a moment, took a letter from his breast-pocket, opened it, and, with a tender smile at his weakness, kissed the writing before restoring it to its place. The letter was one that Anne had written to him at Exeter.

Bob stood perplexed; and then a suspicion crossed his mind that John, from brotherly goodness, might be feigning a satisfaction with recent events which he did not feel. Bob now made a noise with the shutters, at which the trumpet-major rose and went out, Bob at once following him.

'Jack,' said the sailor ingenuously, 'I'm terribly sorry that I've done wrong.'

'How?' asked his brother.

'In courting our little Anne. Well, you see, John, she was in the same house with me, and somehow or other I made myself her beau. But I have been thinking that perhaps you had the first claim on her, and if so, Jack, I'll make way for ye. I—I don't care for her much, you know—not so very much, and can give her up very well. It is nothing serious between us at all. Yes, John, you try to get her ; I can look elsewhere.' Bob never knew how much he loved Anne till he found himself making this speech of renunciation.

'Oh, Bob, you are mistaken !' said the trumpet-major, who was not deceived. ' When I first saw her I admired her, and I admire her now, and like her. I like her so well that I shall be glad to see you marry her.'

' But,' replied Bob, with hesitation, ' I thought I saw you looking very sad, as if you were in love ; I saw you take out a letter, in short. That's what it was disturbed me and made me come to you.'

' Oh, I see your mistake !' said John, laughing forcedly.

At this minute Mrs. Loveday and the miller, who were taking a twilight walk in the garden, strolled round near to where the brothers stood. She talked volubly on events in Weymouth, as most people did at this time. 'And they tell me that the theatre has been painted up afresh,' she was saying, 'and that the actors have come for the season, with the most lovely actresses that ever were seen.'

When they had passed by John continued, 'I *am* in love, Bob; but—not with Anne.'

'Ah! who is it then?' said the mate hopefully.

'One of the actresses at the theatre,' John replied with a concoctive look at the vanishing forms of Mr. and Mrs. Loveday. 'She is a very lovely woman, you know. But we won't say anything more about it—it dashes a man so.'

'Oh, one of the actresses!' said Bob, with open mouth.

'But don't you say anything about it!' continued the trumpet-major heartily. 'I don't want it known.'

'No, no—I won't, of course. May I not know her name?'

'No, not now, Bob. I cannot tell ye,' John answered, and with truth, for Loveday did not know the name of any one actress in the world.

When his brother had gone Captain Bob hastened off in a state of great animation to Anne, whom he found on the top of a neigh-bouring hillock which the daylight had scarcely as yet deserted.

'You have been a long time coming, sir,' said she, in sprightly tones of reproach.

'Yes, dearest; and you'll be glad to hear

why. I've found out the whole mystery—yes —why he's queer, and everything.'

Anne looked startled.

'He's up to the gunnel in love! We must try to help him on in it, or I fear he'll go melancholy-mad like.'

'We help him?' she asked faintly.

'He's lost his heart to one of the play-actresses at Weymouth, and I think she slights him.'

'Oh, I am so glad!' she exclaimed.

'Glad that his venture don't prosper?'

'Oh, no; glad he's so sensible. · How long is it since that alarm of the French?'

'Six weeks, honey. Why do you ask?'

'Men can forget in six weeks, can't they, Bob?'

The impression that John had really kissed her still remained.

'Well, some men might,' observed Bob

judicially. 'I couldn't. Perhaps John might. I couldn't forget *you* in twenty times as long. Do you know, Anne, I half thought it was you John cared about; and it was a weight off my heart when he said he didn't.'

'Did he say he didn't?'

'Yes. He assured me himself that the only person in the hold of his heart was this lovely play-actress, and nobody else.'

'How I should like to see her!'

'Yes. So should I.'

'I would rather it had been one of our own neighbour's girls, whose birth and breeding we know of; but still, if that is his taste, I hope it will end well for him. How very quick he has been! I certainly wish we could see her.'

'I don't know so much as her name. He is very close, and wouldn't tell a thing about her.'

'Couldn't we get him to go to the theatre with us ? and then we could watch him, and easily find out the right one. Then we would learn if she is a good young woman ; and if she is, could we not ask her here, and so make it smoother for him ?   He has been very gay lately ; that means budding love : and sometimes between his gaieties he has had melancholy moments ; that means there's difficulty.'

Bob thought her plan a good one, and resolved to put it in practice on the first available evening.   Anne was very curious as to whether John did really cherish a new passion, the story having quite surprised her.   Possibly it was true ; six weeks had passed since John had shown a single symptom of the old attachment, and what could not that space of time effect in the heart of a soldier whose very profession it was to leave girls behind him ?

After this John Loveday did not come to see them for nearly a month, a neglect which was set down by Bob as an additional proof that his brother's affections were no longer exclusively centred in his old home. When at last he did arrive, and the theatre-going was mentioned to him, the flush of consciousness which Anne expected to see upon his face was unaccountably absent.

'Yes, Bob; I should very well like to go to the theatre,' he replied heartily. 'Who is going besides?'

'Only Anne,' Bob told him, and then it seemed to occur to the trumpet-major that something had been expected of him. He rose and said privately to Bob with some confusion, 'Oh, yes, of course we'll go. As I am connected with one of the—— in short I can get you in for nothing, you know. At least let me manage everything.'

'Yes, yes.  I wonder you didn't propose to take us before, Jack, and let us have a good look at her.'

'I ought to have.  You shall go on a King's night.  You won't want me to point her out, Bob ; I have my reasons at present for asking it ? '

' We'll be content with guessing,' said his brother.

When the gallant John was gone Anne observed, ' Bob, how he is changed !  I watched him.  He showed no feeling, even when you burst upon him suddenly with the subject nearest his heart.'

'It must be because his suit don't fay,' said Captain Bob.

# CHAPTER XXX.

## AT THE THEATRE ROYAL.

In two or three days a message arrived asking them to attend at the theatre on the coming evening, with the added request that they would dress in their gayest clothes, to do justice to the places taken. Accordingly, in the course of the afternoon they drove off, Bob having clothed himself in a splendid suit, recently purchased as an attempt to bring himself nearer to Anne's style when they appeared in public together. As finished off by this dashing and really fashionable attire, he was the perfection of a beau in the dog-days ; pantaloons and boots of the newest make; yards and yards of muslin wound round his neck, forming a sort of asylum for the lower part of his face; two fancy waistcoats, and coat-buttons like circular shaving glasses. The absurd extreme of female fashion, which was to wear muslin dresses in January, was at this time equalled by that of the men, who wore clothes enough in August to melt them. Nobody would have guessed from Bob's presentation now that he had ever been aloft on a dark night in the Atlantic, or knew the hundred ingenuities that could be performed with a rope's end and a marling-spike as well as his mother tongue.

It was a day of days. Anne wore her celebrated celestial blue pelisse, her Leghorn hat, and her muslin dress with the waist under the arms; the latter being decorated with excellent Honiton lace bought of the

woman who travelled from that place to
Overcombe and its neighbourhood with a
basketful of her own manufacture, and a
cushion on which she worked by the wayside.
John met the lovers at the Radipole Inn,
and after stabling the horse they entered the
town together, the trumpet-major informing
them that Weymouth had never been so full
before, that the Court, the Prince of Wales,
and everybody of consequence was there,
and that an attic could scarcely be got for
money. The King had gone for a cruise in
his yacht, and they would be in time to see
him land.

Then drums and fifes were heard, and in
a minute or two they saw Sergeant Stanner
advancing along the street with a firm countenance, fiery poll, and rigid staring eyes, in
front of his recruiting-party. The sergeant's
sword was drawn, and at intervals of two or

three inches along its shining blade were impaled fluttering one-pound notes, to express the lavish bounty that was offered. He gave a stern, suppressed nod of friendship to our people, and passed by. Next they came up to a waggon, bowered over with leaves and flowers, so that the men inside could hardly be seen.

'Come to see the King, hip-hip hurrah!' cried a voice within, and turning they saw through the leaves the nose and face of Cripplestraw. The waggon contained all Derriman's workpeople.

'Is your master here?' said John.

'No, trumpet-major, sir. But young maister is coming to fetch us at nine o'clock, in case we should be too blind to drive home.'

'Oh; where is he now?'

Never mind,' said Anne impatiently, at

which the trumpet-major obediently moved on.

By the time they reached the pier it was six o'clock ; the royal yacht was returning ; a fact announced by the ships in the harbour firing a salute.  The King came ashore with his hat in his hand, and returned the salutations of the well-dressed crowd in his old indiscriminate fashion.  While this cheering and waving of handkerchiefs was going on Anne stood between the two brothers, who protectingly joined their hands behind her back, as if she were a delicate piece of statuary that a push might damage.  Soon the King had passed, and receiving the military salutes of the piquet, joined the Queen and princesses at Gloucester Lodge, the homely house of red brick in which he unostentatiously resided.

As there was yet some little time before

the theatre would open, they strayed upon the velvet sands, and listened to the songs of the saliors, one of whom extemporised for the occasion :

'Portland Road the King aboard, the King aboard !
Portland Road the King aboard,
We weighed and sailed from Portland Road !

When they had looked on awhile at the combats at single-stick which were in progress hard by, and seen the sum of five guineas handed over to the modest gentleman who had broken most heads, they returned to Gloucester Lodge, whence the King and other members of his family now reappeared, and drove, at a slow trot, round to the theatre in carriages drawn by the Hanoverian white horses that were so well known in Weymouth at this date.

When Anne and Bob entered the theatre they found that John had taken excellent

places, and concluded that he had got them
for nothing through the influence of the lady
of his choice. As a matter of fact he had
paid full prices for those two seats, like any
other outsider, and even then had a difficulty
in getting them, it being a King's night.
When they were settled he himself retired
to an obscure part of the pit, from which the
stage was scarcely visible.

'We can see beautifully,' said Bob, in an
aristocratic voice, as he took a delicate pinch
of snuff, and drew out the magnificent pocket-
handkerchief brought home from the East
for such occasions. 'But I am afraid poor
John can't see at all.'

'But we can see him,' replied Anne,
'and notice by his face which of them it is
he is so charmed with. The light of that
corner candle falls right upon his cheek.'

By this time the King had appeared in

his place, which was overhung by a canopy of crimson satin fringed with gold. About twenty places were occupied by the royal family and suite ; and beyond them was a crowd of powdered and glittering personages of fashion, completely filling the centre of the little building; though the King so frequently patronised the local stage during these years that the crush was not inconvenient.

The curtain rose and the play began. To-night it was one of Colman's, who at this time enjoyed great popularity, and Mr. Bannister supported the leading character. Anne, with her hand privately clasped in Bob's, and looking as if she did not know it, partly watched the piece and partly the face of the impressionable John who had so soon transferred his affections elsewhere. She had not long to wait. When a certain one of the subordinate ladies of the comedy entered on the stage the trumpet-major in his corner not only looked conscious, but started and gazed with parted lips.

'This must be the one,' whispered Anne quickly. 'See, he is agitated!'

She turned to Bob, but at the same moment his hand convulsively closed upon hers as he, too, strangely fixed his eyes upon the newly entered lady.

'What is it?'

Anne looked from one to the other without regarding the stage at all. Her answer came in the voice of the actress who now spoke for the first time. The accents were those of Miss Matilda Johnson.

One thought rushed into both their minds on the instant, and Bob was the first to utter it.

'What—is she the woman of his choice after all?'

'If so, it is a dreadful thing!' murmured Anne.

But, as may be imagined, the unfortunate John was as much surprised by this rencounter as the other two. Until this moment he had been in utter ignorance of the theatrical company and all that pertained to it. Moreover, much as he knew of Miss Johnson, he was not aware that she had ever been trained in her youth as an actress, and that after lapsing into straits and difficulties for a couple of years she had been so fortunate as to again procure an engagement here.

The trumpet-major, though not prominently seated, had been seen by Matilda already, who had observed still more plainly her old betrothed and Anne in the other part of the house. John was not concerned on

his own account at being face to face with
her, but at the extraordinary suspicion that
this conjuncture must revive in the minds
of his best beloved friends. After some
moments of pained reflection he tapped his
knee.

'Gad, I won't explain; it shall go as it
is!' he said. 'Let them think her mine.
Better that than the truth, after all.'

Had personal prominence in the scene
been at this moment proportioned to intentness of feeling, the whole audience, regal and
otherwise, would have faded into an indistinct
mist of background, leaving as the sole
emergent and telling figures Bob and Anne
at one point, the trumpet-major on the left
hand, and Matilda at the opposite corner of
the stage. But fortunately the dead-lock of
awkward suspense into which all four had
fallen was terminated by an accident. A

messenger entered the King's box with de-
spatches. There was an instant pause in
the performance. The despatch-box being
opened the King read for a few moments
with great interest, the eyes of the whole
house, including those of Anne Garland,
being anxiously fixed upon his face; for
terrible events fell as unexpectedly as thun-
derbolts at this critical time of our history.
The King at length beckoned to Lord ———,
who was immediately behind him, the play
was again stopped, and the contents of the
despatch were publicly communicated to the
audience.

Sir Robert Calder, cruising off Finisterre,
had come in sight of Villeneuve, and made
the signal for action, which, though checked
by the weather, had resulted in the capture
of two Spanish line-of-battle ships, and the
retreat of Villeneuve into Ferrol.

The news was received with truly national feeling, if noise might be taken as an index of patriotism. 'Rule Britannia' was called for and sung by the whole house. But the importance of the event was far from being recognised at this time; and Bob Loveday, as he sat there and heard it, had very little conception how it would bear upon his destiny.

This parenthetic excitement diverted for a few minutes the eyes of Bob and Anne from the trumpet-major; and when the play proceeded, and they looked back to his corner, he was gone.

'He's just slipped round to talk to her behind the scenes,' said Bob knowingly. 'Shall we go too, and tease him for a sly dog?'

'No, I would rather not.'

'Shall we go home, then?'

'Not unless her presence is too much for you?'

'Oh—not at all. We'll stay here. Ah, there she is again.'

They sat on, and listened to Matilda's speeches, which she delivered with such delightful coolness that they soon began to considerably interest one of the party.

'Well, what a nerve the young woman has!' he said at last in tones of admiration, and gazing at Miss Johnson with all his might. 'After all, Jack's taste is not so bad. She's really deuced clever.'

'Bob, I'll go home if you wish to,' said Anne quickly.

'Oh, no—let us see how she fleets herself off that bit of a scrape she's playing at now. Well, what a hand she is at it, to be sure!'

Anne said no more, but waited on, supremely uncomfortable, and almost tearful.

She began to feel that she did not like life particularly well; it was too complicated: she saw nothing of the scene, and only longed to get away, and to get Bob away with her.   At last the curtain fell on the final act, and then began the farce of *No Song no Supper*.   Matilda did not appear in this piece, and Anne again inquired if they should go home.   This time Bob agreed, and taking her under his care with redoubled affection, to make up for the species of coma which had seized upon his heart for a time, he quietly accompanied her out of the house.

When they emerged upon the esplanade, the August moon was shining across the sea from the direction of St. Alban's Head. Bob unconsciously loitered, and turned towards the pier.   Reaching the end of the promenade they surveyed the quivering waters in silence for some time, until a long dark line shot from behind the promontory of the Nothe, and swept forward into the harbour.

'What boat is that?' said Anne.

'It seems to be from some frigate lying in the Roads,' said Bob carelessly, as he brought Anne round with a gentle pressure of his arm and bent his steps towards the homeward end of the town.

Meanwhile, Miss Johnson, having finished her duties for that evening, rapidly changed her dress, and went out likewise. The prominent position which Anne and Captain Bob had occupied side by side in the theatre, left her no alternative but to suppose that the situation was arranged by Bob as a species of defiance to herself; and her heart, such as it was, became proportionately more embittered against him. In spite of the rise in her fortunes, Miss Johnson still remembered

—and always would remember—her humiliating departure from Overcombe ; and it had been to her even a more grievous thing that Bob had acquiesced in his brother's ruling than that John had determined it. At the time of setting out she was sustained by a firm faith that Bob would follow her, and nullify his brother's scheme ; but though she waited Bob never came.

She passed along by the houses facing the sea, and scanned the shore, the footway, and the open road close to her, which, illuminated by the slanting moon to a great brightness, sparkled with minute facets of crystallised salts from the water sprinkled there during the day. The promenaders at the farther edge appeared in dark profiles ; and beyond them was the grey sea, parted into two masses by the tapering braid of moonlight across the waves.

Two forms crossed this line at a startling nearness to her; she marked them at once as Anne and Bob Loveday. They were walking slowly, and in the earnestness of their discourse were oblivious of the presence of any human beings save themselves. Matilda stood motionless till they had passed.

'How I love them!' she said, treading the initial step of her walk onwards with a vehemence that walking did not demand.

'So do I—especially one,' said a voice at her elbow; and a man wheeled round her, and looked in her face, which had been fully exposed to the moon.

'You—who are you?' she asked.

'Don't you remember, ma'am? We walked some way together towards Overcombe earlier in the summer.' Matilda looked more closely, and perceived that the speaker was Derriman, in plain clothes. He continued, 'You are one of the ladies of the theatre, I know. May I ask why you said in such a queer way that you loved that couple ?'

'In a queer way ?'

'Well, as if you hated them.'

'I don't mind your knowing that I have good reason to hate them. You do, too, it seems ?'

'That man,' said Festus savagely, 'came to me one night about that very woman ; insulted me before I could put myself on my guard, and ran away before I could come up with him and avenge myself. The woman tricks me at every turn. I want to part them.'

'Then why don't you ? There's a splendid opportunity. Do you see that soldier walking along ? He's a marine ; he looks into the gallery of the theatre every night : and

he's in connection with the press-gang that
came ashore just now from the frigate lying
in Portland Roads.    They are often here for
men.'

'Yes.    Our boatmen dread them.'

'Well, we have only to tell him that
Loveday is a seaman to be clear of him this
very night.'

'Done!' said Festus.    'Take my arm
and come this way.'    They walked across to
the footway.    'Fine night, sergeant.'

'It is, sir.'

'Looking for hands, I suppose?'

'It is not to be known, sir.  We don't
begin till half-past ten.'

'It is a pity you don't begin now.    I
could show ye excellent game.'

'What, that little nest of fellows at
the Three Tuns?    I have just heard of
'em.'

'No—come here.' Festus, with Miss Johnson on his arm, led the sergeant quickly along the parade, and by the time they reached the Narrows the lovers, who walked but slowly, were visible in front of them. 'There's your man,' he said.

'That buck in pantaloons and half-boots —a looking like a squire ?'

'Twelve months ago he was mate of the brig *Pewit;* but his father has made money, and keeps him at home.'

'Faith, now you tell of it, there's a hint of sea legs about him. What's the young beau's name ?'

'Don't tell!' whispered Matilda, impulsively clutching Festus's arm.

But Festus had already said, 'Robert Loveday, son of the miller at Overcombe. You may find several likely fellows in that neighbourhood.'

The marine said that he would bear it in mind, and they left him.

'I wish you had not told,' said Matilda. 'She's the worst.'

'Dash my eyes now; listen to that! Why, you chicken-hearted old stager, you was as well agreed as I. Come now; hasn't he used you badly?'

Matilda's acrimony returned. 'I was down on my luck, or he wouldn't have had the chance,' she said.

'Well, then, let things be.'

# CHAPTER XXXI.

### MIDNIGHT VISITORS.

MISS GARLAND and Loveday walked leisurely to the inn and called for horse-and-gig. While the hostler was bringing it round, the landlord, who knew Bob and his family well, spoke to him quietly in the passage.

'Is this then because you want to throw dust in the eyes of the *Black Diamond* chaps?' (with an admiring glance at Bob's costume).

'The *Black Diamond?*' said Bob; and Anne turned pale.

'She hove in sight just after dark, and at nine o'clock a boat having more than a dozen marines on board, with cloaks on, rowed into harbour.'

Bob reflected. 'Then there'll be a press to-night; depend upon it,' he said.

'They won't know you, will they Bob?' said Anne, anxiously.

'They certainly won't know him for a seaman now,' remarked the landlord, laughing, and again surveying Bob up and down. 'But if I was you two, I should drive home along straight and quiet; and be very busy in the mill all to-morrow, Mr. Loveday.'

They drove away; and when they had got onward out of the town, Anne strained her eyes wistfully towards Portland. Its dark contour, lying like a whale on the sea, was just perceptible in the gloom as the background to half-a-dozen ships' lights nearer at hand.

'They can't make you go, now you are

a gentleman tradesman, can they?' she
asked.

'If they want me they can have me,
dearest. I have often said I ought to volunteer.'

'And not care about me at all?'

'It is just that that keeps me at home. I
won't leave you if I can help it.'

'It cannot make such a vast difference to
the country whether one man goes or stays!
But if you want to go you had better, and not
mind us at all!'

Bob put a period to her speech by a mark
of affection to which history affords many
parallels in every age. She said no more
about the *Black Diamond*; but whenever
they ascended a hill she turned her head to
look at the lights in Portland Roads, and the
grey expanse of intervening sea.

Though Captain Bob had stated that he
did not wish to volunteer, and would not
leave her if he could help it, the remark
required some qualification. That Anne was
charming and loving enough to chain him
anywhere was true ; but he had begun to find
the mill-work terribly irksome at times. Often
during the last month, when standing among
the rumbling cogs in his new miller's suit,
which ill became him, he had yawned, thought
wistfully of the old pea-jacket, and the waters
of the deep blue sea. His dread of displeasing
his father by showing anything of this change
of sentiment was great ; yet he might have
braved it but for knowing that his marriage
with Anne, which he hoped might take place
the next year, was dependent entirely upon
his adherence to the mill business. Even
were his father indifferent, Mrs. Loveday

would never intrust her only daughter to the hands of a husband who would be away from home five-sixths of his time.

But though, apart from Anne, he was not averse to seafaring in itself, to be smuggled thither by the machinery of a press-gang was intolerable ; and the process of seizing, stunning, pinioning, and carrying off unwilling hands was one which Bob as a man had always determined to hold out against to the utmost of his power.   Hence, as they went towards home, he frequently listened for sounds behind him, but hearing none he assured his sweetheart that they were safe for that night at least.   The mill was still going when they arrived, though old Mr. Loveday was not to be seen ; he had retired as soon as he heard the horse's hoofs in the lane leaving Bob to watch the grinding till three o'clock ; when the elder would rise, and

Bob withdraw to bed—a frequent arrangement between them since Bob had taken the place of grinder.

Having reached the privacy of her own room, Anne threw open the window, for she had not the slightest intention of going to bed just yet. The tale of the *Black Diamond* had disturbed her by a slow, insidious process that was worse than sudden fright. Her window looked into the court before the house, now wrapped in the shadow of the trees and the hill; and she leaned upon its sill listening intently. She could have heard any strange sound distinctly enough in one direction; but in the other all low noises were absorbed in the patter of the mill, and the rush of water down the race.

However, what she heard came from the hitherto silent side, and was intelligible in a moment as being the footsteps of men. She tried to think they were some late stragglers from Weymouth. Alas! no ; the tramp was too regular for that of villagers. She hastily turned, extinguished the candle, and listened again. As they were on the main road there was, after all, every probability that the party would pass the bridge which gave access to the mill court without turning in upon it, or even noticing that such an entrance existed. In this again she was disappointed : they crossed into the front without a pause. The pulsations of her heart became a turmoil now, for why should these men, if they were the press-gang, and strangers to the locality, have supposed that a sailor was to be found here, the younger of the two millers Loveday being never seen now in any garb which could suggest that he was other than a miller pure, like his father. One of the men spoke.

'I am not sure that we are in the right place,' he said.

'This is a mill, anyhow,' said another.

'There's lots about here.'

'Then come this way a moment with your light.'

Two of the group went towards the cart-house on the opposite side of the yard, and when they reached it a dark lantern was opened, the rays being directed upon the front of the miller's waggon.

'"Loveday and Son, Overcombe Mill,"' continued the man, reading from the waggon. '"Son," you see, is lately painted in.   That's our man.'

He moved to turn off the light, but before he had done so it flashed over the forms of the speakers, and revealed a sergeant, a naval officer, and a file of marines.

Anne waited to see no more.   When Bob

stayed up to grind, as he was doing to-night, he often sat in his room instead of remaining all the time in the mill; and this room was an isolated chamber over the bakehouse, which could not be reached without going down-stairs and ascending the step-ladder that served for his staircase. Anne descended in the dark, clambered up the ladder, and saw that light strayed through the chink below the door. His window faced towards the garden, and hence the light could not as yet have been seen by the press-gang.

'Bob, dear Bob!' she said, through the keyhole. 'Put out your light, and run out of the back-door!'

'Why?' said Bob, leisurely knocking the ashes from the pipe he had been smoking.

'The press-gang!'

'They have come? By gad! who can

have blown upon me ? All right, dearest.
I'm game.'

Anne, scarcely knowing what she did,
descended the ladder and ran to the back-
door, hastily unbolting it to save Bob's time,
and gently opening it in readiness for him.
She had no sooner done this than she felt
hands laid upon her shoulder from without,
and a voice exclaiming, 'That's how we doos
it—quite an obleeging young man !'

Though the hands held her rather roughly,
Anne did not mind for herself, and turning she
cried desperately, in tones intended to reach
Bob's ears : 'They are at the back-door ;
try the front !'

But inexperienced Miss Garland little
knew the shrewd habits of the gentlemen she
had to deal with, who, well-used to this sort of
pastime, had already posted themselves at
every outlet from the premises.

'Bring the lantern,' shouted the fellow who held her. 'Why—'tis a girl! I half thought so.—Here is a way in,' he continued to his comrades, hastening to the foot of the ladder which led to Bob's room.

'What d'ye want?' said Bob, quietly opening the door, and showing himself still radiant in the full dress that he had worn with such effect at Weymouth, which he had been about to change for his mill suit when Anne gave the alarm.

'This gentleman can't be the right one,' observed a marine, rather impressed by Bob's appearance.

'Yes, yes; that's the man,' said the sergeant. 'Now take it quietly, my young cock-o'-wax. You look as if you meant to, and 'tis wise of ye.'

'Where are you going to take me?' said Bob.

'Only aboard the *Black Diamond*. If you choose to take the bounty and come voluntarily you'll be allowed to go ashore whenever your ship's in port. If you don't, and we've got to pinion ye, you will not have your liberty at all. As you must come, willy-nilly, you'll do the first if you've any brains whatever.'

Bob's temper began to rise. 'Don't you talk so large, about your pinioning, my man. When I've settled——'

'Now or never, young blow-hard,' interrupted his informant.

'Come, what jabber is this going on?' said the lieutenant, stepping forward. 'Bring your man.'

One of the marines set foot on the ladder, but at the same moment a shoe from Bob's hand hit the lantern with well-aimed directness, knocking it clean out of the grasp of the

man who held it.   In spite of the darkness
they began to scramble up the ladder.   Bob
thereupon shut the door, which being but of
slight construction, was as he knew only a
momentary defence.   But it gained him time
enough to open the window, gather up his
legs upon the sill, and spring across into the
apple-tree growing without.   He alighted
without much hurt beyond a few scratches
from the boughs, a shower of falling apples
testifying to the force of his leap.

‘ Here he is !’ shouted several below who
had seen Bob’s figure flying like a raven’s
across the sky.

There was stillness for a moment in the
tree.   Then the fugitive made haste to climb
out upon a low-hanging branch towards the
garden, at which the men beneath all rushed
in that direction to catch him as he dropped,
saying, ‘You may as well come down, old

boy. 'Twas a spry jump, and we give ye credit for 't.'

The latter movement of Loveday had been a mere feint. Partly hidden by the leaves he glided back to the other part of the tree, from whence it was easy to jump upon a thatch-covered out-house. This intention they did not appear to suspect, which gave him the opportunity of sliding down the slope and entering the back-door of the mill.

'He's here, he's here!' the men exclaimed, running back from the tree.

By this time they had obtained another light, and pursued him closely along the back quarters of the mill. Bob had entered the lower room, seized hold of the chain by which the flour-sacks were hoisted from story to story by connection with the mill-wheel, and pulled the rope that hung alongside for the purpose of throwing it into gear. The

foremost pursuers arrived just in time to see
Captain Bob's legs and shoe-buckles vanishing through the trap-door in the joists over-
head, his person having been whirled up by
the machinery like any bag of flour, and the
trap falling to behind him.

'He's gone up by the hoist!' said the
sergeant, running up the ladder in the corner
to the next floor, and elevating the light just
in time to see Bob's suspended figure ascending in the same way through the same sort of
trap into the second floor. The second trap
also fell together behind him, and he was lost
to view as before.

It was more difficult to follow now; there
was only a flimsy little ladder, and the man
ascended cautiously. When they stepped
out upon the loft it was empty.

'He must ha' let go here,' said one of the
marines, who knew more about mills than the

others. ' If he had held fast a moment longer he would have been dashed against that beam.'

They looked up. The hook by which Bob had held on had ascended to the roof, and was winding round the cylinder. Nothing was visible elsewhere but boarded divisions like the stalls of a stable, on each side of the stage they stood upon, these compartments being more or less heaped up with wheat and barley in the grain.

' Perhaps he's buried himself in the corn.'

The whole crew jumped into the corn-bins, and stirred about their yellow contents ; but neither arm, leg, nor coat-tail was uncovered. They removed sacks, peeped among the rafters of the roof, but to no purpose. The lieutenant began to fume at the loss of time.

' What cursed fools to let the man go !

Why, look here, what's this?' He had opened the door by which sacks were taken in from waggons without, and dangling from the cat-head projecting above it was the rope used in lifting them. 'There's the way he went down,' the officer continued. 'The man's gone.'

Amidst mumblings and curses the gang descended the pair of ladders and came into the open air; but Captain Bob was nowhere to be seen. When they reached the front door of the house the miller was standing on the threshold, half dressed.

'Your son is a clever fellow, miller,' said the lieutenant; 'but it would have been much better for him if he had come quiet.'

'That's a matter of opinion,' said Loveday.

'I have no doubt that he's in the house.'

'He may be ; and he may not.'

' Do you know where he is ?'

' I do not ; and if I did I shouldn't tell.'

' Naturally.'

' I heard steps beating up the road, sir,' said the sergeant.

They turned from the door, and leaving four of the marines to keep watch round the house, the remainder of the party marched into the lane as far as where the other road branched off. While they were pausing to decide which course to take one of the soldiers held up the light. A black object was discernible upon the ground before them, and they found it to be a hat—the hat of Bob Loveday.

' We are on the track,' cried the sergeant, deciding for this direction.

They tore on rapidly, and the footsteps previously heard became audible again, increasing in clearness, which told that they gained upon the fugitive, who in another five minutes stopped and turned. The rays of the candle fell upon Anne.

'What do you want?' she said, showing her frightened face.

They made no reply, but wheeled round and left her. She sank down on the bank to rest, having done all she could. It was she who had taken down Bob's hat from a nail, and dropped it at the turning with the view of misleading them till he should have got clear off.

## CHAPTER XXXII.

### DELIVERANCE.

BUT Anne Garland was too anxious to remain long away from the centre of operations. When she got back she found that the press-gang were standing in the court discussing their next move.

'Waste no more time here,' the lieutenant said. 'Two more villages to visit to-night, and the nearest three miles off. There's nobody else in this place, and we can't come back again.'

When they were moving away one of the private marines, who had kept his eye on Anne, and noticed her distress, contrived to say in a whisper as he passed her, ' We are coming back again as soon as it begins to get light ; that's only said to deceive ye. Keep your young man out of the way.'

They went as they had come ; and the little household then met together, Mrs Loveday having by this time dressed herself and come down. A long and anxious discussion followed.

' Somebody must have told upon the chap,' Loveday remarked. ' How should they have found him out else, now he's been home from sea this twelvemonth ? '

Anne then mentioned what the friendly marine had told her ; and fearing lest Bob was in the house, and would be discovered there when daylight came, they searched and called for him everywhere.

' What clothes has he got on ? ' said the miller.

'His lovely new suit,' said his wife. 'I warrant it is quite spoiled!'

'He's got no hat,' said Anne.

'Well,' said Loveday, 'you two go and lie down now and I'll bide up; and as soon as he comes in, which he'll do most likely in the course of the night, I'll let him know that they are coming again.'

Anne and Mrs. Loveday went to their bedrooms, and the miller entered the mill as if he were simply staying up to grind. But he continually left the flour-shoot to go outside and walk round; each time he could see no living being near the spot. Anne meanwhile had lain down dressed upon her bed, the window still open, her ears intent upon the sound of footsteps, and dreading the reappearance of daylight and the gang's return. Three or four times during the night she descended to the mill to inquire of her step-

father if Bob had shown himself ; but the
answer was always in the negative.

At length the curtains of her bed began to
reveal their pattern, the brass handles of
the drawers gleamed forth, and day dawned.
While the light was yet no more than a suf-
fusion of pallor, she arose, put on her hat, and
determined to explore the surrounding premises before the men arrived. Emerging
into the raw loneliness of the daybreak, she
went upon the bridge and looked up and
down the road. It was as she had left it,
empty, and the solitude was rendered yet
more insistent by the silence of the mill-
wheel, which was now stopped, the miller
having given up expecting Bob and retired
to bed about three o'clock. The footprints
of the marines still remained in the dust on
the bridge, all the heel-marks towards the

house, showing that the party had not as yet returned.

While she lingered she heard a slight noise in the other direction, and, turning, saw a woman approaching. The woman came up quickly, and, to her amazement, Anne recognised Matilda. Her walk was convulsive, face pale, almost haggard, and the cold light of the morning invested it with all the ghostliness of death. She had plainly walked all the way from Weymouth, for her shoes were covered with dust.

'Has the press-gang been here?' she gasped. 'If not they are coming!'

'They have been.'

'And got him?—I am too late!'

'No; they are coming back again. Why did you——'

'I came to try to save him. Can we save him? Where is he?'

Anne looked the woman in the face, and it was impossible to doubt that she was in earnest.

'I don't know.' she answered. 'I am trying to find him before they come.'

'Will you not let me help you?' cried the repentant Matilda.

Without either objecting or assenting Anne turned and led the way to the back part of the homestead.

Matilda, too, had suffered that night. From the moment of parting with Festus Derriman a sentiment of revulsion from the act to which she had been a party set in and increased, till at length it reached an intensity of remorse which she could not passively bear. She had risen before day and hastened thitherward to know the worst, and if possible hinder consequences that she had been the first to set in train.

After going hither and thither in the adjoining field, Anne entered the garden. The walks were bathed in grey dew, and as she passed observantly along them it appeared as if they had been brushed by some foot at a much earlier hour. At the end of the garden, bushes of broom, laurel, and yew formed a constantly encroaching shrubbery, that had come there almost by chance, and was never trimmed. Behind these bushes was a garden-seat, and upon it lay Bob sound asleep.

The ends of his hair were clotted with damp, and there was a foggy film upon the mirror-like buttons of his coat, and upon the buckles of his shoes. His bunch of new gold seals was dimmed by the same insidious dampness; his shirt-frill and muslin neckcloth were limp as seaweed. It was plain that he had been there a long time. Anne shook him, but he did not awake, his breathing being slow and stertorous.

'Bob, wake; 'tis your own Anne!' she said, with innocent earnestness; and then, fearfully turning her head, she saw that Matilda was close behind her.

'You needn't mind me,' said Matilda, bitterly. 'I am on your side now. Shake him again.'

Anne shook him again, but he slept on. Then she noticed that his forehead bore the mark of a heavy wound.

'I fancy I hear something!' said her companion, starting forward and endeavouring to wake Bob herself. 'He is stunned, or drugged!' she said; 'there is no rousing him.'

Anne raised her head and listened. From the direction of the eastern road came the sound of a steady tramp. 'They are coming back !' she said, clasping her hands. 'They will take him, ill as he is! He won't open his eyes—no, it is no use! Oh, what shall we do ?'

Matilda did not reply, but running to the end of the seat on which Bob lay, tried its weight in her arms.

'It is not too heavy,' she said. 'You take that end, and I'll take this. We'll carry him away to some place of hiding.'

Anne instantly seized the other end, and they proceeded with their burden at a slow pace to the lower garden-gate, which they reached as the tread of the press-gang re-sounded over the bridge that gave access to the mill court, now hidden from view by the hedge and the trees of the garden.

'We will go down inside this field,' said Anne, faintly.

'No!' said the other; 'they will see our

foot-tracks in the dew.   We must go into the road.'

'It is the very road they will come down when they leave the mill.'

'It cannot be helped; it is nick or nothing with us now.'

So they emerged upon the road, and staggered along without speaking, occasionally resting for a moment to ease their arms; then shaking him to arouse him, and finding it useless, seizing the seat again.   When they had gone about two hundred yards Matilda betrayed signs of exhaustion, and she asked, 'Is there no shelter near?'

'When we get to that little field of corn,' said Anne.

'It is so very far.   Surely there is some place near?'

She pointed to a few scrubby bushes

overhanging a little stream, which passed under the road near this point.

'They are not thick enough,' said Anne.

'Let us take him under the bridge,' said Matilda. 'I can go no farther.'

Entering the opening by which cattle descended to drink, they waded into the weedy water, which here rose a few inches above their ankles. To ascend the stream, stoop under the arch, and reach the centre of the roadway, was the work of a few minutes.

'If they look under the arch we are lost,' murmured Anne.

'There is no parapet to the bridge, and they may pass over without heeding.'

They waited, their heads almost in contact with the reeking arch, and their feet encircled by the stream, which was at its summer lowness now. For some minutes

they could hear nothing but the babble of the
water over their ankles, and round the legs
of the seat on which Bob slumbered, the
sounds being reflected in a musical tinkle
from the hollow sides of the arch.   Anne's
anxiety now was lest he should not continue
sleeping till the search was over, but start up
with his habitual imprudence, and scorning
such means of safety, rush out into their
arms.

A quarter of an hour dragged by, and
then indications reached their ears that the
re-examination of the mill had begun and
ended.   The well-known tramp drew nearer,
and reverberated through the ground over
their heads, where its volume signified to the
listeners that the party had been largely aug-
mented by pressed men since the night
preceding.   The gang passed the arch, and
the noise regularly diminished, as if no man

among them had thought of looking aside for a moment.

Matilda broke the silence. 'I wonder if they have left a watch behind?' she said, doubtfully.

'I will go and see,' said Anne. 'Wait till I return.'

'No; I can do no more. When you come back I shall be gone. I ask one thing of you. If all goes well with you and him, and he marries you—don't be alarmed; my plans lie elsewhere—when you are his wife tell him who helped to carry him away. But don't mention my name to the rest of your family, either now or at any time.'

Anne regarded the speaker for a moment, and promised; after which she waded out from the archway.

Matilda stood looking at Bob for a moment, as if preparing to go, till moved by some impulse she bent and lightly kissed him once.

' How can you ! ' cried Anne, reproachfully. When leaving the mouth of the arch she had bent back and seen the act.

Matilda flushed. ' You jealous baby ! ' she said scornfully.

Anne hesitated for a moment, then went out from the water, and hastened towards the mill.

She entered by the garden, and, seeing no one, advanced and peeped in at the window. Her mother and Mr. Loveday were sitting within as usual.

' Are they all gone ? ' said Anne softly.

' Yes. They did not trouble us much, beyond going into every room, and searching about the garden, where they saw steps. They have been lucky to-night ; they have caught fifteen or twenty men at places farther on; so the loss of Bob was no hurt to their feelings. I wonder where in the world the poor fellow is!'

'I will show you,' said Anne. And explaining in a few words what had happened, she was promptly followed by David and Loveday along the road. She lifted her dress and entered the arch with some anxiety on account of Matilda; but the actress was gone, and Bob lay on the seat as she had left him.

Bob was brought out, and water thrown upon his face; but though he moved he did not rouse himself until some time after he had been borne into the house. Here he opened his eyes, and saw them standing round, and gathered a little consciousness.

'You are all right, my boy!' said his father. 'What hev happened to ye? Where did ye get that terrible blow?'

'Ah—I can mind now,' murmured Bob,
with a stupefied gaze around. 'I fell in
slipping down the topsail halyard—the rope,
that is, was too short— and I fell upon my
head. And then I went away. When I
came back I thought I wouldn't disturb ye :
so I lay down out there, to sleep out the
watch ; but the pain in my head was so great
that I couldn't get to sleep ; so I picked
some of the poppy-heads in the border,
which I once heard was a good thing for
sending folks to sleep when they are in pain.
So I munched up all I could find, and
dropped off quite nicely.'

'I wondered who had picked 'em !' said
Molly.   'I noticed they were gone.'

'Why, you might never have woke
again !' said Mrs Loveday, holding up her
hands.   'How is your head now ? '

'I hardly know,' replied the young man,

putting his hand to his forehead and beginning to doze again. 'Where be those fellows that boarded us? With this—smooth water and—fine breeze we ought to get away from 'em. Haul in—the larboard braces, and—bring her to the wind.'

'You are at home, dear Bob,' said Anne, bending over him, 'and the men are gone.'

'Come along up-stairs: th' beest hardly awake now,' said his father; and Bob was assisted to bed.

# CHAPTER XXXIII.

## A DISCOVERY TURNS THE SCALE.

In four-and-twenty hours Bob had recovered. But though physically himself again, he was not at all sure of his position as a patriot. He had that practical knowledge of seamanship of which the country stood much in need, and it was humiliating to find that impressment seemed to be necessary to teach him to use it for her advantage. Many neighbouring young men, less fortunate than himself, had been pressed and taken; and their absence seemed a reproach to him. He went away by himself into the mill-roof, and, surrounded by the corn-heaps, gave vent to self-condemnation.

'Certainly, I am no man to lie here so long for the pleasure of sighting that young girl forty times a day, and letting her sight me—bless her eyes !—till I must needs want a press-gang to teach me what I've forgot. And is it then all over with me as a British sailor ?  We'll see.'

When he was thrown under the influence of Anne's eyes again, which were more tantalisingly beautiful than ever just now (so it seemed to him), his intention of offering his services to the Government would wax weaker, and he would put off his final decision till the next day.  Anne saw these fluctuations of his mind between love and patriotism, and being terrified by what she had heard of sea-fights, used the utmost art of which she was capable to seduce him from his forming purpose. She came to him in the mill, wearing the very prettiest of her morning jackets—the one that only just passed the waist, and was laced so tastefully round the collar and bosom. Then she would appear in her new hat, with a bouquet of primroses on one side; and on the following Sunday she walked before him in lemon-coloured boots, so that her feet looked like a pair of yellow-hammers flitting under her dress.

But dress was the least of the means she adopted for chaining him down. She talked more tenderly than ever; asked him to begin small undertakings in the garden on her account; she sang about the house, that the place might seem cheerful when he came in. This singing for a purpose required great effort on her part, leaving her afterwards very sad. When Bob asked her what was the matter, she would say, ' Nothing ; only I am thinking how you will grieve your father, and cross his purposes, if you carry out your unkind notion of going to sea, and forsaking your place in the mill.'

' Yes,' Bob would say, uneasily. ' It will trouble him, I know.'

Being also quite aware how it would trouble her, he would again postpone, and thus another week passed away.

All this time John had not come once to the mill. It appeared as if Miss Johnson absorbed all his time and thoughts. Bob was often seen chuckling over the circumstance. ' A sly rascal !' he said. ' Pretending on the day she came to be married that she was not good enough for me, when it was only that he wanted her for himself. How he could have persuaded her to go away is beyond me to say !'

Anne could not contest this belief of her lover's, and remained silent; but there had more than once occurred to her mind a doubt of its probability. Yet she had only abandoned her opinion that John had schemed for Matilda, to embrace the opposite error; that, finding he had wronged the young lady, he had pitied and grown to love her.

'And yet Jack, when he was a boy, was the simplest fellow alive,' resumed Bob. 'By George, though, I should have been hot against him for such a trick, if in losing her I hadn't found a better! But she'll never come down to him in the world; she has high notions now. I am afraid he's doomed to sigh in vain!'

Though Bob regretted this possibility, the feeling was not reciprocated by Anne. It was true that she knew nothing of Matilda's temporary treachery, and that she disbelieved

the story of her lack of virtue; but she did
not like the woman. 'Perhaps it will not
matter if he is doomed to sigh in vain,' she
said. 'But I owe him no ill-will. I have
profited by his doings, incomprehensible as
they are.' And she bent her fair eyes on
Bob and smiled.

Bob looked dubious. 'He thinks he has
affronted me, now I have seen through him,
and that I shall be against meeting him.
But, of course, I am not so touchy. I can
stand a practical joke, as can any man who
has been afloat. I'll call and see him, and
tell him so.'

Before he started, Bob bethought him of
something which would still further prove to
the misapprehending John that he was entirely forgiven. He went to his room, and
took from his chest a packet containing a
lock of Miss Johnson's hair, which she had

given him during their brief acquaintance,
and which till now he had quite forgotten.
When, at starting, he wished Anne good-
bye, it was accompanied by such a beaming
face, that she knew he was full of an idea,
and asked what it might be that pleased
him so.

'Why, this,' he said, smacking his breast-
pocket. 'A lock of hair that Matilda gave
me.'

Anne sank back with parted lips.

'I am going to give it to Jack—he'll jump
for joy to get it! And it will show him how
willing I am to give her up to him, fine piece
as she is.'

'Will you see her to-day, Bob?' Anne
asked with an uncertain smile.

'Oh, no—unless it is by accident.'

On reaching Radipole he went straight to
the barracks, and was lucky enough to find

John in his room, at the left-hand corner of
the quadrangle. John was glad to see him ;
but to Bob's surprise he showed no imme-
diate contrition, and thus afforded no room
for the brotherly speech of forgiveness which
Bob had been going to deliver. As the
trumpet-major did not open the subject, Bob
felt it desirable to begin himself.

'I have brought ye something that you
will value, Jack,' he said, as they sat at the
window, overlooking the large square barrack
yard. 'I have got no further use for it, and
you should have had it before if it had
entered my head.'

'Thank you, Bob ; what is it ?' said John,
looking absently at an awkward squad of
young men who were drilling in the enclosure.

''Tis a young woman's lock of hair.'

'Ah !' said John, quite recovering from
his abstraction, and slightly flushing. Could

Bob and Anne have quarrelled? Bob drew
the paper from his pocket, and opened it.

'Black!' said John.

'Yes—black enough.'

'Whose?'

'Why, Matilda's.'

'Oh, Matilda's!'

'Whose did you think then?'

Instead of replying, the trumpet-major's
face became as red as sunset, and he turned
to the window to hide his confusion.

Bob was silent, and then he, too, looked
into the court. At length he arose, walked
to his brother, and laid his hand upon his
shoulder. 'Jack,' he said, in an altered voice,
'you are a good fellow. Now I see it all.'

'Oh, no—that's nothing,' said John,
hastily.

'You've been pretending that you care
for this woman that I mightn't blame myself

for heaving you out from the other—which is what I've done without knowing it.'

'What does it matter?'

'But it does matter! I've been making you unhappy all these weeks and weeks through my thoughtlessness. They seemed to think at home, you know, John, that you had grown not to care for her; or I wouldn't have done it for all the world!'

'You stick to her, Bob, and never mind me. She belongs to you. She loves you. I have no claim upon her, and she thinks nothing about me.'

'She likes you, John, thoroughly well; so does everybody; and if I hadn't come home, putting my foot in it—— That coming home of mine has been a regular blight upon the family! I ought never to have stayed. The sea is my home, and why couldn't I bide there?'

The trumpet-major drew Bob's discourse off the subject as soon as he could, and Bob, after some unconsidered replies and remarks, seemed willing to avoid it for the present. He did not ask John to accompany him home, as he had intended; and on leaving the barracks turned southward and entered the town to wander about till he could decide what to do.

It was the 3rd of September, but Weymouth still retained its summer aspect. The King's bathing-machine had been drawn out just as Bob reached Gloucester Buildings, and he waited a minute, in the lack of other distraction, to look on. Immediately that the King's machine had entered the water a group of florid men with fiddles, violoncellos, a trombone, and a drum, came forward, packed themselves into another machine that was in waiting, and were drawn out into the waves in the King's rear. All that was to be heard for a few minutes were the slow pulsations of the sea ; and then a deafening noise burst from the interior of the second machine with power enough to split the boards asunder ; it was the condensed mass of musicians inside, striking up the strains of 'God save the King,' as his Majesty's head rose from the water. Bob took off his hat and waited till the end of the perform-ance, which, intended as a pleasant surprise to George III. by the loyal burghers, he probably tolerated rather than desired. Loveday then passed on to the harbour, where he remained awhile, looking at the busy scene of loading and unloading craft, swabbing the decks of yachts ; at the boats and barges rubbing against the quay wall, and at the green-shuttered houses of the Weymouth merchants, with their heavy

wooden bow-windows which appeared as if
about to drop into the harbour by their own
weight.   All these things he gazed upon, and
thought of one thing—that he had caused
great misery to his brother John.

The town clock struck, and Bob retraced
his steps till he again approached the Esplanade and Gloucester Lodge, where the morning sun blazed in upon the house fronts, and
not a spot of shade seemed to be attainable.
A huzzaing attracted his attention, and he
observed that a number of people had
gathered before the King's residence, where a
brown curricle had stopped, out of which
stepped a hale man in the prime of life, wearing a blue uniform, gilt epaulettes, cocked
hat, and sword, who crossed the pavement and
went in.   Bob went up and joined the group.
'What's going on ?' he said.

'Captain Hardy,' replied a bystander.

' What of him ? '

' Just gone in—waiting to see the King.'

' But he's in the West Indies ? '

' No. The fleet is come home ; they can't find the French anywhere.'

' Will they go and look for them again ? ' asked Bob.

' Oh, yes. Nelson is determined to find 'em. As soon as he's refitted he'll put to sea again. Ah, here's the King coming in.'

Bob was so interested in what he had just heard that he scarcely noticed the arrival of the King, and a body of attendant gentlemen. He went on thinking of his new knowledge ; Captain Hardy was come. He was doubt-less staying with his family at Portisham, a few miles from Overcombe, where he usually spent the intervals between his different cruises.

Loveday returned to the mill without

further delay; and shortly explaining that
John was very well, and would come soon,
went on to talk of the arrival of Nelson's
captain.

'And is he come at last?' said the miller,
throwing his thoughts years backward.
'Well can I mind when he first left home
to go on board the "Helena" as mid-
shipman!'

'That's not much to remember. I can
remember it too,' said Mrs. Loveday.

''Tis more than twenty years ago anyhow.
And more than that, I can mind when he was
born; I was a lad, serving my 'prenticeship
at the time. He has been in this house often
and often when 'a was young. When he
came home after his first voyage he stayed
about here a long time, and used to look
in at the mill whenever he went past. "What
will you be next, sir?" said mother to him

one day as he stood with his back to the door-post. "A lieutenant, Dame Loveday," says he. "And what next?" says she. "A commander." "And next?" "Next, post-captain." "And then?" "Then it will be almost time to die." I'd warrant that he'd mind it to this very day if you were to ask him.'

Bob heard all this with a manner of pre-occupation, and soon retired to the mill. Thence he went to his room by the back passage, and taking his old seafaring gar-ments from a dark closet in the wall conveyed them to the loft at the top of the mill, where he occupied the remaining spare moments of the day in brushing the mildew from their folds, and hanging each article by the window to get aired. In the evening he returned to the loft, and dressing himself in the old salt suit, went out of the house unobserved by anybody, and ascended the road towards Portisham.

The bare downs were now brown with the droughts of the passing summer, and few living things met his view, the natural rotundity of the elevation being only occasionally disturbed by the presence of a barrow, a thorn-bush, or a piece of dry wall which remained from some attempted enclosure.   By the time that he reached the village it was dark, and the larger stars had begun to shine when he walked up to the door of the old-fashioned house which was the family residence of the Hardys.

'Will the Captain allow me to wait on him to-night?' inquired Loveday, explaining who and what he was.

The servant went away for a few minutes, and then told Bob that he might see the Captain in the morning.

'If that's the case, I'll come again,' replied Bob, quite cheerful that failure was not absolute.

He had left the door but a few steps when he was called back and asked if he had walked all the way from Overcombe Mill on purpose.

Loveday replied modestly that he had done so.

'Then will you come in?' He followed the speaker into a small study or office, and in a minute or two Captain Hardy entered.

The Captain at this time was a bachelor of thirty-five, rather stout in build, with light eyes, bushy eyebrows, a square broad face, plenty of chin, and a mouth whose corners played between humour and grimness. He surveyed Loveday from top to toe.

'Robert Loveday, sir, son of the miller at Overcombe,' said Bob, making a low bow.

'Ah! I remember your father, Loveday,' the gallant seaman replied. 'Well, what do you want to say to me?' Seeing that Bob found it rather difficult to begin, he leant leisurely against the mantel-piece, and went on, 'Is your father well and hearty? I have not seen him for many, many years.'

'Quite well, thank ye.'

'You used to have a brother in the army, I think? What was his name—John? A very fine fellow, if I recollect.'

'Yes; he's there still.'

'And you are in the merchant-service?'

'Late first mate of the brig "Pewit."'

'How is it you're not on board a man-of-war?'

'Ay, sir, that's the thing I've come about,' said Bob, recovering confidence. 'I should have been, but I've waited and waited on at home because of a young woman—

lady, I might have said, for she's sprung from a higher class of society than I. Her father was a landscape painter—maybe you've heard of him, sir? The name is Garland.'

'He painted that view of Portisham,' said Captain Hardy, looking towards a dark little picture in the corner of the room.

Bob looked, and went on, as if to the picture, 'Well, sir, I have found that—— However, the press-gang came a week or two ago, and didn't get hold of me. I didn't care to go aboard as a pressed man.'

'There has been a severe impressment. It is of course a disagreeable necessity, but it can't be helped.'

'Since then, sir, something has happened that makes me wish they had found me, and I have come to-night to ask if I could enter on board your ship the "Victory."'

The Captain shook his head severely, and presently observed : ' I am glad to find that you think of entering the service, Loveday ; smart men are badly wanted. But it will not be in your power to choose your ship.'

' Well, well, sir ; then I must take my chance elsewhere,' said Bob, his face indicating the disappointment he would not fully express. ''Twas only that I felt I would much rather serve under you than anybody else, my father and all of us being known to ye, Captain Hardy, and our families belonging to the same parts.'

Captain Hardy took Bob's altitude more carefully. ' Are you a good practical seaman ? ' he asked, musingly.

' Ay, sir ; I believe I am.'

' Active ?  Fond of skylarking ? '

' Well, I don't know about the last.  I think I can say I am active enough.  I could

walk the yard-arm, if required, cross from
mast to mast by the stays, and do what most
fellows do who call themselves spry.'

The Captain then put some questions
about the details of navigation, which Loveday, having luckily been used to square rigs,
answered satisfactorily. 'As to reefing topsails,' he added, 'if I don't do it like a flash
of lightning, I can do it so that they will
stand blowing weather. The "Pewit" was not
a dull vessel, and when we were convoyed
home from Lisbon, she could keep well in
sight of the frigate scudding at a distance,
by putting on full sail. We had enough
hands aboard to reef topsails man-o'-war
fashion, which is a rare thing in these days,
sir, now that able seamen are so scarce on
trading craft. And I hear that men from
square-rigged vessels are liked much the best
in the navy, as being more ready for use. So

that I shouldn't be altogether so raw,' said Bob earnestly, 'if I could enter on your ship, sir.    Still, if I can't, I can't.'

'I might ask for you, Loveday,' said the Captain, thoughtfully, 'and so get you there that way.    In short, I think I may say I will ask for you.    So consider it settled.'

'My thanks, to you, sir,' said Loveday.

'You are aware that the "Victory" is a smart ship, and that cleanliness and order are, of necessity, more strictly insisted upon there than in some others?'

'Sir, I quite see it.'

'Well, I hope you will do your duty as well on a line-of-battle ship as you did when mate of the brig, for it is a duty that may be serious.'

Bob replied that it should be his one endeavour; and receiving a few instructions for getting on board the guard-ship, and

being conveyed to Portsmouth, he turned to
go away.

'You'll have a stiff walk before you fetch
Overcombe Mill this dark night, Loveday,'
concluded the Captain, peering out of the
window. 'I'll send you in a glass of grog to
help ye on your way.'

The Captain then left Bob to himself, and
when he had drunk the grog that was brought
in he started homeward, with a heart not exactly light, but large with a patriotic cheer-
fulness, which had not diminished when, after
walking so fast in his excitement as to be
beaded with perspiration, he entered his
father's door.

They were all sitting up for him, and at
his approach anxiously raised their sleepy
eyes, for it was nearly eleven o'clock.

'There ; I knew he'd not be much longer !'
cried Anne, jumping up and laughing, in her

relief. 'They have been thinking you were very strange and silent to day, Bob; you were not, were you?'

'What's the matter, Bob?' said the miller; for Bob's countenance was sublimed by his recent interview, like that of a priest just come from the *penetralia* of the temple.

'He's in his mate's clothes, just as when he came home,' observed Mrs. Loveday.

They all saw now that he had something to tell. 'I am going away,' he said when he had sat down. 'I am going to enter on board a man-of-war, and perhaps it will be the "Victory."'

'Going?' said Anne, faintly.

'Now, don't you mind it, there's a dear,' he went on solemnly, taking her hand in his own. 'And you, father, don't you begin to take it to heart' (the miller was looking grave). 'The press-gang has been here, and though I showed them that I was a free man, I am going to show everybody that I can do my duty.'

Neither of the other three answered, Anne and the miller having their eyes bent upon the ground, and the former trying to repress her tears.

'Now don't you grieve, either of you,' he continued ; 'nor vex yourselves that this has happened. Please not to be angry with me, father, for deserting you and the mill, where you want me, for I *must go*. For these three years we and the rest of the country have been in fear of the enemy ; trade has been hindered ; poor folk made hungry ; and many rich folk made poor. There must be a deliverance, and it must be done by sea. I have seen Captain Hardy, and I shall serve under him if so be I can.'

'Captain Hardy ? '

'Yes. I have been to Portisham, walked there and back, and I wouldn't have missed it for fifty guineas. I hardly thought he would see me; but he did see me. And he hasn't forgot you."

Bob then opened his tale in order, relating graphically the conversation to which he had been a party, and they listened with breathless attention.

'Well, if you must go, you must,' said the miller with emotion; 'but I think it somewhat hard that, of my two sons, neither one of 'em can be got to stay and help me in my business as I get old.'

'Don't trouble and vex about it,' said Mrs. Loveday, soothingly. 'They are both instruments in the hands of Providence, chosen to chastise that Corsican ogre, and do what they can for the country in these trying years.'

'That's just the shape of it, Mrs. Loveday,' said Bob.

'And he'll come back soon,' she continued, turning to Anne. 'And then he'll tell us all he has seen, and the glory that he's won, and how he has helped to sweep that scourge Buonaparty off the earth.'

'When be you going, Bob?' his father inquired.

'To-morrow, if I can. I shall call at the barracks and tell John as I go by. When I get to Portsmouth——"

A burst of sobs in quick succession interrupted his words; they came from Anne, who till that moment had been sitting as before with her hand in that of Bob, and apparently quite calm. Mrs. Loveday jumped up, but before she could say anything to soothe the agitated girl she had calmed herself with the same singular suddenness that had marked her giving way. 'I don't mind Bob's going,' she said. 'I think he ought to go. Don't suppose, Bob, that I want you to stay!'

After this she left the apartment, and went into the little side room where she and her mother usually worked. In a few moments Bob followed her. When he came back he was in a very sad and emotional mood. Anybody could see that there had been a parting of profound anguish to both.

'She is not coming back to-night,' he said.

'You will see her to-morrow before you go?' said her mother.

'I may or I may not,' he replied. 'Father and Mrs. Loveday, do you go to bed now. I have got to look over my things and get ready; and it will take me some little time. If you should hear noises you will know it is only myself moving about.'

When Bob was left alone he suddenly became brisk, and set himself to overhaul his clothes and other possessions in a business-like manner. By the time that his chest was packed, such things as he meant to leave at home folded into cupboards, and what was useless destroyed, it was past two o'clock. Then he went to bed, so softly that only the creak of one weak stair revealed his passage upward. At the moment that he passed Anne's chamber-door her mother was bending over her as she lay in bed, and saying to her, 'Won't you see him in the morning?'

'No, no,' said Anne. 'I would rather not see him. I have said that I may. But I shall not. I cannot see him again.'

When the family got up next day Bob

had vanished. It was his way to disappear like this, to avoid affecting scenes at parting. By the time that they had sat down to a gloomy breakfast, Bob was in the boat of a Weymouth waterman, who pulled him along-side the guard-ship in the roads, where he laid hold of the man-rope, mounted, and dis-appeared from external view. In the course of the day the ship moved off, set her royals, and made sail for Portsmouth, with five hun-dred new hands for the service on board, consisting partly of pressed men and partly of volunteers, among the latter being Robert Loveday.

## CHAPTER XXXIV.

### A SPECK ON THE SEA.

IN parting from John, who accompanied him to the quay, Bob had said : ' Now, Jack, these be my last words to you : I give her up. I go away on purpose, and I shall be away a long time. If in that time she should list over towards ye ever so little, mind you take her. You have more right to her than I. You chose her when my mind was elsewhere, and you best deserve her ; for I have never known you forget one woman, while I've forgot a dozen. Take her then, if she will come, and God bless both of ye.'

Another person besides John saw Bob

go. That was Derriman, who was standing
by a bollard a little farther up the quay. He
did not repress his satisfaction at the sight.
John looked towards him with an open gaze
of contempt; for the cuffs administered to
the yeoman at the inn had not, so far as the
trumpet-major was aware, produced any desire to avenge that insult, John being, of
course, quite ignorant that Festus had erro-
neously retaliated upon Bob, in his peculiar
though scarcely soldierly way. Finding that
he did not even now approach him, John
went on his way, and thought over his intention of preserving intact the love between
Anne and his brother.

He was surprised when he next went to
the mill to find how glad they all were to see
him. From the moment of Bob's return to
the bosom of the deep Anne had had no exist-
ence on land; people might have looked at

her human body and said she had flitted thence. The sea and all that belonged to the sea was her daily thought and her nightly dream. She had the whole two-and-thirty winds under her eye, each passing gale that ushered in returning autumn being mentally registered ; and she acquired a precise knowledge of the direction in which Portsmouth, Brest, Ferrol, Cadiz, and other such likely places lay. Instead of saying her own familiar prayers at night she substituted, with some confusion of thought, the Forms of Prayer to be used at sea. John at once noticed her lorn, abstracted looks, pitied her, —how much he pitied her !—and asked when they were alone if there was anything he could do.

'There are two things,' she said, with almost childish eagerness in her tired eyes.

'They shall be done.'

'The first is to find out if Captain Hardy
has gone back to his ship; and the other is
—oh, if you will do it, John!—to get me
newspapers whenever possible.'

After this dialogue John was absent for
a space of three hours, and they thought he
had gone back to barracks.  He entered,
however, at the end of that time, took off his
forage-cap, and wiped his forehead.

'You look tired, John,' said his father.

'Oh no.'   He went through the house
till he had found Anne Garland.

'I have only done one of those things,' he
said to her.

'What, already?   I didn't hope for or
mean to-day.'

'Captain Hardy is gone from Portisham.
He left some days ago.   We shall soon hear
that the fleet has sailed.'

'You have been all the way to Portisham on purpose. How good of you!'

'Well, I was anxious to know myself when Bob is likely to leave. I expect now that we shall soon hear from him.'

Two days later he came again. He brought a newspaper, and what was better, a letter for Anne, franked by the first lieutenant of the 'Victory.'

'Then he's aboard her,' said Anne, as she eagerly took the letter.

It was short, but as much as she could expect in the circumstances, and informed them that the captain had been as good as his word, and had gratified Bob's earnest wish to serve under him. The ship, with Admiral Lord Nelson on board, and accompanied by the frigate 'Euryalus,' was to sail in two days for Plymouth, where they would be joined by others, and thence proceed to the coast of Spain.

Anne lay awake that night thinking of the 'Victory,' and of those who floated in her. To the best of Anne's calculation that ship of war would, during the next twenty-four hours, pass within a few miles of where she herself then lay. Next to seeing Bob, the thing that would give her more pleasure than any other in the world was to see the vessel that contained him—his floating city, his sole dependence in battle and storm—upon whose safety from winds and enemies hung all her hope.

The next day was Weymouth market, and in this she saw her opportunity. A carrier went from Overcombe at six o'clock, and having to do a little shopping for herself in Weymouth, she gave it as a reason for her intended day's absence, and took a place in the van. When she reached the town it was still early morning, but the borough was already in the zenith of its daily bustle and show. The King was always out-of-doors by six o'clock, and such cock-crow hours at Gloucester Lodge produced an equally forward stir among the population. She alighted, and passed down the esplanade, as fully thronged by persons of fashion at this time of mist and level sunlight as a watering-place in the present day is at four in the afternoon. Dashing bucks and beaux in cocked hats, black feathers, ruffles, and frills, stared at her as she hurried along ; the beach was swarming with bathing women, wearing waistbands that bore the national refrain, ' God save the King' in gilt letters ; the shops were all open, and Sergeant Stanner, with his sword-stuck bank-notes and heroic gaze, was beating up at two guineas and a crown, the crown to drink his Majesty's health.

She soon finished her shopping, and then, crossing over into the old town, pursued her way along the coast-road to Portland. At the end of an hour she had been rowed across the Fleet (which then lacked the convenience of a bridge), and reached the base of Portland Hill. The steep incline before her was dotted with houses, showing the pleasant peculiarity of one man's doorstep being behind his neighbour's chimney, and slabs of stone as the common material for walls, roof, floor, pig-stye, stable-manger, door-scraper, and garden-stile. Anne gained the summit, and followed along the central track over the huge lump of freestone which forms the peninsula, the wide sea prospect extending as she went on. Weary with her journey, she approached the extreme south-

erly peak of rock, and gazed from the cliff at
Portland Bill.

The wild, herbless, weather-worn promontory was quite a solitude, and, saving the one
old lighthouse about fifty yards up the slope,
scarce a mark was visible to show that
humanity had ever been near the spot. Anne
found herself a seat on a stone, and swept
with her eyes the tremulous expanse of water
around her that seemed to utter a cease-
less unintelligible incantation. Out of the
three hundred and sixty degrees of her
complete horizon two hundred and fifty were
covered by waves, the *coup d'œil* including the
area of troubled waters known as the Race,
where two seas met to effect the destruction
of such vessels as could not be mastered by
one. She counted the craft within her view :
there were five ; no, there were only four ; no,

there were seven, some of the specks having resolved themselves into two. They were all small coasters, and kept well within sight of land.

Anne sank into a reverie. Then she heard a slight noise on her left-hand, and turning beheld an old sailor, who had approached with a glass. He was levelling it over the sea in a direction to the south-east, and somewhat removed from that in which her own eyes had been wandering. Anne moved a few steps thitherward, so as to unclose to her view a deeper sweep on that side, and by this discovered a ship of far larger size than any which had yet dotted the main before her. Its sails were for the most part new and clean, and in comparison with its rapid progress before the wind the small brigs and ketches seemed standing still.

Upon this striking object the old man's glass was bent.

'What do you see, sailor?' she asked.

'Almost nothing,' he answered. 'My sight is so gone off lately that things, one and all, be but a November mist to me. And yet I fain would see to-day. I am looking for the "Victory."'

'Why?' she said, quickly.

'I have a son aboard her. He's one of three from these parts. There's the captain, there's my son Ned, and there's young Loveday of Overcombe—he that lately joined.'

'Shall I look for you?' said Anne, after a pause.

'Certainly, mis'ess, if so be you please.'

Anne took the glass, and he supported it by his arm. 'It is a large ship,' she said, 'with three masts, three rows of guns along the side, and all her sails set.'

' I guessed as much.'

' There is a little flag in front—over her bowsprit.'

' The jack ? '

' And there's a large one flying at her stern.'

' The ensign.'

' And a white one on her fore-topmast.'

' That's the admiral's flag, the flag of my Lord Nelson.  What is her figure-head, my dear ? '

' A coat-of-arms, supported on this side by a sailor.'

Her companion nodded with satisfaction. ' On the other side of that figure-head is a marine.'

' She is twisting round in a curious way, and her sails sink in like old cheeks, and she shivers like a leaf upon a tree.'

' She is in stays, for the larboard tack.    I

can see what she's been doing. She's been re'ching close in to avoid the flood tide, as the wind is to the sou'-west, and she's bound down ; but as soon as the ebb made, d'ye see, they made sail to the west'ard. Captain Hardy may be depended upon for that ; he knows every current about here, being a native.'

'And now I can see the other side : it is a soldier where a sailor was before. You are *sure* it is the " Victory ?" '

' I am sure.'

After this a frigate came into view—the ' Euryalus '—sailing in the same direction. Anne sat down, and her eyes never left the ships. ' Tell me more about the " Victory," ' she said.

' She is the best sailor in the service, and she carries a hundred guns. The heaviest be on the lower deck, the next size on the middle deck, the next on the main and upper decks. My son Ned's place is on the lower deck, because he's short, and they put the short men below.'

Bob, though not tall, was not likely to be specially selected for shortness. She pictured him on the upper deck, in his snow-white trousers and jacket of navy blue, looking perhaps towards the very point of land where she then was.

The great silent ship, with her population of blue jackets, marines, officers, captain, and the admiral who was not to return alive, passed like a phantom the meridian of the Bill. Sometimes her aspect was that of a large white bat, sometimes that of a grey one. In the course of time the watching girl saw that the ship had passed her nearest point; the breadth of her sails diminished by fore-shortening, till she assumed the form of an egg on end. After this something seemed to twinkle, and Anne, who had previously with-drawn from the old sailor, went back to him, and looked again through the glass. The twinkling was the light falling upon the cabin windows of the ship's stern. She ex-plained it to the old man.

'Then we see now what the enemy have seen but once. That was in seventy-nine, when she sighted the French and Spanish fleet off Scilly, and she retreated because she feared a landing. Well, 'tis a brave ship, and she carries brave men!'

Anne's tender bosom heaved, but she said nothing, and again became absorbed in con-templation.

The 'Victory' was fast dropping away. She was on the horizon, and soon appeared hull down. That seemed to be like the beginning of a greater end than her present

vanishing.  Anne Garland could not stay by
the sailor any longer, and went about a
stone's throw off, where she was hidden by
the inequality of the cliff from his view.  The
vessel was now exactly end on, and stood
out in the direction of the Start, her width
having contracted to the proportion of a
feather.  She sat down again, and mechani-
cally took out some biscuits that she had
brought, foreseeing that her waiting might
be long.  But she could not eat one of them ;
eating seemed to jar with the mental tense-
ness of the moment ; and her undeviating
gaze continued to follow the lessened ship
with the fidelity of a balanced needle to a
magnetic stone, all else in her being motionless.

The courses of the 'Victory' were
absorbed into the main, then her topsails
went, and then her top-gallants.  She was

now no more than a dead fly's wing on a sheet of spider's web; and even this frag-ment diminished. Anne could hardly bear to see the end, and yet she resolved not to flinch. The admiral's flag sank behind the watery line, and in a minute the very truck of the last topmast stole away. The 'Victory' was gone.

Anne's lip quivered as she murmured, without removing her wet eyes from the vacant and solemn horizon, ' " They that go down to the sea in ships, that do business in great waters——" '

' " These see the works of the Lord, and His wonders in the deep," ' was returned by a man's voice from behind her.

Looking round quickly, she saw a soldier standing there ; and the grave eyes of John Loveday bent on her.

''Tis what I was thinking,' she said, trying to be composed.

'You were saying it,' he answered, gently.

'Was I ?—I did not know it. . . . How came you here ?' she presently added.

'I have been behind you a good while; but you never turned round.'

'I was deeply occupied,' she said, in an undertone.

'Yes—I too came to see him pass. I heard this morning that Lord Nelson had embarked, and I knew at once that they would sail immediately. The 'Victory' and 'Euryalus' are to join the rest of the fleet at Plymouth. There was a great crowd of people assembled to see the admiral off; they cheered him and the ship as she dropped down. He took his coffin on board with him, they say.'

'His coffin ?' said Anne, turning deadly

pale.   'Something terrible, then, is meant by
that!   Oh, why *would* Bob go in that ship?
—doomed to destruction from the very beginning like this!'

'It was his determination to sail under
Captain Hardy, and under no one else,' said
John.   'There may be hot work; but we
must hope for the best.'   And observing how
wretched she looked, he added, 'But won't
you let me help you back?   If you can walk
as far as Church-Hope Cove it will be enough.
A lerret is going from there to Weymouth
Harbour in the course of an hour; it belongs
to a man I know, and they can take one pas-
senger, I am sure.'

She turned her back upon the Channel,
and by his help soon reached the place indi-
cated.   The boat was lying there as he had
said.   She found it to belong to the old man
who had been with her at the Bill, and was

in charge of his two younger sons. The trumpet-major helped her into it over the slippery blocks of stone, one of the young men spread his jacket for her to sit on, and as soon as they pulled from shore John climbed up the blue-grey cliff, and disappeared over the top, to return to Weymouth by the Chesil Road.

Anne was in the town by three o'clock. The trip in the stern of the lerret had quite refreshed her, with the help of the biscuits, which she had at last been able to eat. The van from Weymouth to Overcombe did not start till four o'clock, and feeling no further interest in the gaieties of the place, she strolled on through Radipole, her mind settling down again upon the possibly sad fate of the 'Victory' when she found herself alone. She did not hurry on; and finding that even now there wanted another half-hour to the carrier's time, she turned into a little lane to escape the inspection of the numerous passers-by. Here all was quite lonely and still, and she sat down under a willow-tree, absently regarding the landscape, which had now begun to put on the rich tones of declining summer, but which to her was as hollow and faded as a theatre by day. She could hold out no longer ; burying her face in her hands, she wept without restraint.

Some yards behind her was a little spring of water, having a stone margin round it to prevent the cattle from treading in the sides and filling it up with dirt. While she wept two elderly gentlemen entered unperceived upon the scene, and walked on to the spring's brink. Here they paused and looked in, afterwards moving round it, and then stooping as if to smell or taste its waters. The spring was, in fact, a sulphurous one, then

recently discovered by a physician who lived
in the neighbourhood ; and it was beginning
to attract some attention, having by common
report contributed to effect such wonderful
cures as almost passed belief.  After a con-
siderable discussion, apparently on how the
pool might be improved for better use, one
of the two elderly gentlemen turned away,
leaving the other still probing the spring
with his cane.  The first stranger, who wore
a blue coat with gilt buttons, came on in the
direction of Anne Garland, and seeing her
sad posture went quickly up to her, and said
abruptly, ' What is the matter ? '

Anne, who in her grief had observed
nothing of the gentlemen's presence, withdrew her handkerchief from her eyes and
started to her feet.  She instantly recognised
her interrogator as the King.

' What, crying ?' his Majesty inquired, kindly. ' How is this ? '

' I—have seen a dear friend go away, sir,' she faltered, with downcast eyes.

' Ah !—partings are sad—very sad—for us all. You must hope your friend will return soon. Where is he or she gone ? '

' I don't know, your Majesty.'

' Don't know—how is that ? '

' He is a sailor on board the " Victory." '

'Then he has reason to be proud,' said the King with interest. ' He is your brother ? '

Anne tried to explain what he was, but could not, and blushed with painful heat.

' Well, well, well ; what is his name ? '

' In spite of Anne's confusion and low spirits, her natural woman's shrewdness told her at once that no harm could be done

by revealing Bob's name; and she answered,
' His name is Robert Loveday, sir.'

' Loveday—a good name. I shall not
forget it. Now dry your cheeks, and don't
cry any more. Loveday—Robert Loveday.'

Anne curtseyed, the King smiled good-
humouredly, and turned to rejoin his companion, who was afterwards heard to be
Dr.——, the physician in attendance at
Gloucester Lodge. This gentleman had in
the meantime filled a small phial with the
medicinal water, which he carefully placed
in his pocket; and on the King coming up
they retired together and disappeared.
Thereupon Anne, now thoroughly aroused,
followed the same way with a gingerly tread,
just in time to see them get into a carriage
which was in waiting at the turning of the
lane.

She quite forgot the carrier, and everything else in connection with riding home. Flying along the road rapidly and unconsciously, when she awoke to a sense of her whereabouts she was so near to Overcombe as to make the carrier not worth waiting for. She had been borne up in this hasty spurt at the end of a weary day by visions of Bob promoted to the rank of admiral, or something equally wonderful, by the King's special command, the chief result of the promotion being, in her arrangement of the piece, that he would stay at home and go to sea no more. But she was not a girl who indulged in extravagant fancies long, and before she reached home she thought that the King had probably forgotten her by that time, and her troubles, and her lover's name.

# CHAPTER XXXV.

## A SAILOR ENTERS.

THE remaining fortnight of the month of September passed away, with a general decline from the summer's excitements. The Royal family left Weymouth the first week in October, the German Legion with their artillery about the same time. The dragoons still remained at Radipole barracks, and John Loveday brought to Anne every newspaper that he could lay hands on, especially such as contained any fragment of shipping news. This threw them much together; and at these times John was often awkward and confused, on account of the unwonted stress of concealing his great love for her.

Her interests had grandly developed from the limits of Overcombe and Weymouth life to an extensiveness truly European. During the whole month of October, however, not a single grain of information reached her, or anybody else, concerning Nelson and his blockading squadron off Cadiz. There were the customary bad jokes about Buonaparte, especially when it was found that the whole French army had turned its back upon Boulogne and set out for the Rhine. Then came accounts of his march through Germany and into Austria; but not a word about the 'Victory.'

At the beginning of autumn John brought news which fearfully depressed her. The Austrian General Mack had capitulated with his whole army. Then were revived the

old misgivings as to invasion. 'Instead of
having to cope with him weary with waiting,
we shall have to encounter This Man fresh
from the fields of victory,' ran the newspaper
article.

But the week which had led off with such
a dreary piping was to end in another key.
On the very day when Mack's army was
piling arms at the feet of its conqueror, a
blow had been struck by Bob Loveday and
his comrades which eternally shattered the
enemy's force by sea. Four days after the
receipt of the Austrian news Corporal Tul-
lidge ran into the miller's house to inform
him that on the previous Monday, at eleven
in the morning, the 'Pickle' schooner, Lieutenant Lapenotiere, had arrived at Falmouth
with dispatches from the fleet; that the
stage-coaches on the highway from Exeter to
London were chalked with the words 'Great

Victory!' 'Glorious Triumph!' and so on; and that all the country people were wild to know particulars.

On Friday afternoon John arrived with authentic news of the battle off Cape Trafalgar, and the death of Nelson. Captain Hardy was alive; he had escaped with the loss of his shoe-buckle. But it was feared that the 'Victory' had been the scene of the heaviest slaughter among all the ships engaged, though as yet no returns of killed and wounded had been issued, beyond a rough list of the numbers in some of the ships.

The suspense of the little household in Overcombe Mill was great in the extreme. John came thither daily for more than a week; but no further particulars reached England till the end of that time, and then only the meagre intelligence that there had been a gale immediately after the battle, and that many of the prizes had been lost. Anne said little to all these things, and preserved a superstratum of calmness on her countenance ; but some inner voice seemed to whisper to her that Bob was no more. Miller Loveday drove to Portisham several times to learn if the Captain's sisters had received any more definite tidings than these flying reports ; but that family had heard nothing which could in any way relieve the miller's anxiety. When at last, at the end of November, there appeared a final and revised list of killed and wounded as issued by Admiral Collingwood, it was a useless sheet to the Lovedays. To their great pain it contained no names but those of officers, the friends of ordinary seamen and marines being on that occasion left to discover their losses as best they might.

Anne's conviction of her loss increased

with the darkening of the early winter days.
Bob was not a cautious man who would
avoid needless exposure, and a hundred and
fifty of the 'Victory's' crew had been disabled
or slain. Anybody who had looked into her
room at this time would have seen that her
favourite reading was the office for the Burial
of the Dead at Sea, beginning 'We therefore
commit his body to the deep.' In these first
days of December several of the victorious
fleet came into port; but not the 'Victory.'
Many supposed that that noble ship, disabled
by the battle, had gone to the bottom in the
subsequent tempestuous weather; and the
belief was persevered in till it was told in
Weymouth that she had been seen passing up
the Channel. Two days later the 'Victory'
arrived at Portsmouth.

Then letters from survivors began to
appear in the public prints which John so

regularly brought to Anne; but though he watched the mails with unceasing vigilance there was never a letter from Bob. It sometimes crossed John's mind that his brother might still be alive and well, and that in his wish to abide by his expressed intention of giving up Anne and home life he was deliberately lax in writing. If so, Bob was carrying out the idea too thoughtlessly by half, as could be seen by watching the effects of suspense upon the fair face of the victim, and the anxiety of the rest of the family.

It was a clear day in December. The first slight snow of the season had been sifted over the earth, and one side of the apple-tree branches in the miller's garden was touched with white, though a few leaves were still lingering on the tops of the younger trees. A short sailor of the royal navy, who was not Bob, or anything like him, crossed the mill

court and came to the door. The miller
hastened out and brought him into the room,
where John, Mrs. Loveday, and Anne Garland were all present.

'I'm from aboard the "Victory," said the
sailor. 'My name's Jim Cornick. And
your lad is alive and well.'

They breathed rather than spoke their
thankfulness and relief, the miller's eyes being
moist as he turned aside to calm himself;
while Anne, having first jumped up wildly
from her seat, sank back again under the
almost insupportable joy that trembled
through her limbs to her utmost finger.

'I've come from Spithead to Portisham,'
the sailor continued, 'and now I am going
on to father at Weymouth.'

'Ah—I know your father,' cried the
trumpet-major, 'old James Cornick.'

It was the man who had brought Anne in his lerret from Portland Bill.

'And Bob hasn't got a scratch?' said the miller.

'Not a scratch,' said Cornick.

Loveday then bustled off to draw the visitor something to drink. Anne Garland, with a glowing blush on her face, had gone to the back part of the room, where she was the very embodiment of sweet content as she slightly swayed herself without speaking. A little tide of happiness seemed to ebb and flow through her in listening to the sailor's words, moving her figure with it. The seaman and John went on conversing.

'Bob had a good deal to do with barricading the hawse-holes afore we were in action, and the adm'l and cap'n both were very much pleased at how 'twas done. When the adm'l went up the quarter-deck ladder Cap'n

Hardy said a word or two to Bob, but what it was I don't know, for I was quartered at a gun some ways off. However, Bob saw the adm'l stagger when 'a was wownded, and was one of the men who carried him to the cockpit. After that he and some other lads jumped aboard the French ship, and I believe they was in her when she struck her flag. What 'a did next I can't say, for the wind had dropped, and the smoke was like a cloud. But 'a got a good deal talked about; and they say there's promotion in store for'n.'

At this point in the story Jim Cornick stopped to drink, and a low unconscious humming came from Anne in her distant corner; the faint melody continued more or less when the conversation between the sailor and the Lovedays was renewed.

'We heard afore that the " Victory " was near knocked to pieces,' said the miller.

'Knocked to pieces? You'd say so if so be you could see her. Gad, her sides be battered like an old penny piece; the shot be still sticking in her wales, and her sails be like so many clap-nets: we have run all the way home under jury top-masts; and as for her decks, you may swab wi' hot water, and you may swab wi' cold; but there's the blood stains, and there they'll bide. . . . The cap'n had a narrow escape, like many o' the rest—a shot shaved his ankle like a razor. You should have seen that man's face in the het o' battle, his features were as if they'd been cast in steel.'

'We rather expected a letter from Bob before this.'

'Well,' said Jim Cornick, with a smile of toleration, 'you must make allowances. The truth o't is, he's engaged just now at Portsmouth, like a good many of the rest from our ship. . . . 'Tis a very nice young woman that he's a courting of, and I make no doubt that she'll be an excellent wife for him.'

'Ah!' said Mrs. Loveday, in a warning tone.

'Courting—wife?' said the miller.

They instinctively looked towards Anne. Anne had started as if shaken by an invisible hand, and a thick mist of doubt seemed to obscure the intelligence of her eyes. This was but for two or three moments. Very pale, she arose and went right up to the seaman. John gently tried to intercept her, but she passed him by.

'Do you speak of Robert Loveday as courting a wife?' she asked, without the least betrayal of emotion.

'I didn't see you, miss,' replied Cornick, turning. 'Yes, your brother hev' his eye on a wife, and he deserves one.   I hope you don't mind ? '

'Not in the least,' she said, with a stage laugh.   'I am interested, naturally.   And what is she ? '

'A very nice young master-tailor's daughter, honey.   A very wise choice of the young man's.'

' Is she fair or dark ? '

' Her hair is rather light.'

' I like light hair ; and her name ? '

' Her name is Caroline.   But can it be that my story hurts ye ?   If so——'

'Yes, yes,' said John, interposing anxiously.   'We don't care for more just at this moment.'

'We *do* care for more,' said Anne, vehemently.   'Tell it all, sailor.   That is a very pretty name, Caroline.   When are they going to be married ? '

'I don't know as how the day is settled,' answered Jim, even now scarcely conscious of the devastation he was causing in one fair breast. 'But from the rate the courting is scudding along at, I should say it won't be long first.'

'If you see him when you go back give him my best wishes,' she lightly said, as she moved away. 'And,' she added, with solemn bitterness, 'say that I am glad to hear he is making such good use of the first days of his escape from the Valley of the Shadow of Death!' She went away, expressing indifference by audibly singing in the distance—

'Shall we go dance the round, the round, the round,
Shall we go dance the round?'

'Your sister is lively at the news,' observed Jim Cornick.

'Yes,' murmured John gloomily, as he

gnawed his lower lip and kept his eyes fixed on the fire.

'Well,' continued the man from the 'Victory,' 'I won't say that your brother's intended ha'n't got some ballast, which is very lucky for'n, as he might have picked up with a girl without a single copper nail. To be sure there was a time we had when we got into port! It was open house for us all!' And after mentally regarding the scene for a few seconds Jim emptied his cup and rose to go.

The miller was saying some last words to him outside the house, Anne's voice had hardly ceased singing up-stairs, John was standing by the fireplace, and Mrs. Loveday was crossing the room to join her daughter, whose manner had given her some uneasiness, when a noise came from above the ceiling, as of some heavy body falling. Mrs. Loveday rushed to the staircase, saying,

'Ah, I feared something!' and she was followed by John.

When they entered Anne's room, which they both did almost at one moment, they found her lying insensible upon the floor. The trumpet-major, his lips tightly closed, lifted her in his arms, and laid her upon the bed; after which he went back to the door to give room to her mother, who was bending over the girl with some hartshorn.

Presently Mrs. Loveday looked up and said to him, 'She is only in a faint, John, and her colour is coming back. Now leave her to me; I will be down-stairs in a few minutes, and tell you how she is.'

John left the room. When he gained the lower apartment his father was standing by the chimney-piece, the sailor having gone. The trumpet-major went up to the fire, and, grasping the edge of the high chimney-shelf, stood silent.

'Did I hear a noise when I went out?' asked the elder, in a tone of misgiving.

'Yes, you did,' said John. 'It was she, but her mother says she is better now. Father,' he added impetuously, 'Bob is a worthless blockhead! If there had been any good in him he would have been drowned years ago!'

'John, John—not too fast,' said the miller. 'That's a hard thing to say of your brother, and you ought to be ashamed of it.'

'Well, he tries me more than I can bear. Good heaven! what can a man be made of to go on as he does? Why didn't he come home; or if he couldn't get leave why didn't he write? 'Tis scandalous of him to serve a woman like that.'

'Gently, gently. The chap hev done

his duty as a sailor ; and though there might have been something between him and Anne, her mother, in talking it over with me, ias said many times that she couldn't think of their marrying till Bob had settled down in business with me. Folks that gain vic-tories must have a little liberty allowed 'em. Look at the admiral himself, for that matter.'

John continued looking at the red coals, till hearing Mrs. Loveday's foot on the stair-case, he went to meet her.

'She is better,' said Mrs. Loveday ; · but she won't come down again to-day.'

Could John have heard what the poor girl was moaning to herself at that moment as she lay writhing on the bed, he would have doubted her mother's assurance : 'If he had been dead I could have borne it, but this I cannot bear!'

## CHAPTER XXXVI.

### DERRIMAN SEES CHANCES.

MEANWHILE Sailor Cornick had gone on his
way as far as the forking roads, where he
met Festus Derriman on foot. The latter
attracted by the seaman's dress, and by
seeing him come from the mill, at once
accosted him. Jim, with the greatest readiness, fell into conversation, and told the same
story as that he had related at the mill.

'Bob Loveday going to be married?' repeated Festus.

'You all seem struck of a heap wi' that.'

'No; I never heard news that pleased
me more.'

When Cornick was gone Festus, instead
of passing straight on, halted on the little
bridge and meditated.  Bob, being now interested elsewhere, would probably not resent
the siege of Anne's heart by another ; there
could, at any rate, be no further possibility of
that looming duel which had troubled the
yeoman's mind ever since his horse-play on
Anne at the house on the down.  To march
into the mill and propose to Mrs. Loveday
for Anne before John's interest could revive
in her was, to this hero's thinking, excellent
discretion.

The day had already begun to darken
when he entered, and the cheerful fire shone
red upon the floor and walls.  Mrs. Loveday
received him alone, and asked him to take
a seat by the chimney-corner, a little of the
old hankering for him as a son-in-law having
permanently remained with her.

'Your servant, Mrs. Loveday,' he said, 'and I will tell you at once what I come for. You will say that I take time by the forelock when I inform you that it is to push on my long-wished-for ailiance wi' your daughter, as I believe she is now a free woman again.'

'Thank you, Mr. Derriman,' said the mother placably. 'But she is ill at present. I'll mention it to her when she is better.'

'Ask her to alter her cruel, cruel resolves against me, on the score of—of my consuming passion for her. In short,' continued Festus, dropping his parlour language in his warmth, 'I'll tell thee what, Dame Loveday, I want the maid, and must have her.'

Mrs. Loveday replied that that was very plain speaking.

'Well, 'tis. But Bob has given her up. He never meant to marry her. I'll tell you,

Mrs. Loveday, what I have never told a soul before.   I was standing upon Weymouth Quay on that very day in last September that Bob set sail, and I heard him say to his brother John that he gave your daughter up.'

'Then it was very unmannerly of him to trifle with her so,' said Mrs. Loveday, warmly.   'Who did he give her up to?'

Festus replied with hesitation, 'He gave her up to John.'

'To John?   How could he give her up to a man already over head and ears in love with that actress woman?'

'Oh!   You surprise me.   Which actress is it?'

'That Miss Johnson!   Anne tells me that he loves her hopelessly.'

Festus arose.   Miss Johnson seemed suddenly to acquire high value as a sweetheart

at this announcement. He had himself felt
a nameless attractiveness in her, and John
had done likewise. John crossed his path
in all possible ways.

Before the yeoman had replied somebody
opened the door, and the firelight shone
upon the uniform of the person they dis-
cussed. Festus nodded on recognising him,
wished Mrs. Loveday good evening, and
went out precipitately.

' So Bob told you he meant to break off
with my Anne when he went away ?' Mrs.
Loveday remarked to the trumpet-major.
' I wish I had known of it before.'

John appeared disturbed at the sudden
charge. He murmured that he could not
deny it, and then hastily turned from her
and followed Derriman, whom he saw before
him on the bridge.

' Derriman !' he shouted.

Festus started and looked round. 'Well, trumpet-major,' he said, blandly.

'When will you have sense enough to mind your own business, and not come here telling things you have heard by sneaking behind people's backs?' demanded John, hotly. 'If you can't learn in any other way, I shall have to pull your ears again, as I did the other day!'

'*You* pull my ears? How can you tell that lie, when you know 'twas somebody else pulled 'em?'

'Oh no, no. I pulled your ears, and thrashed you in a mild way.'

'You'll swear to it? Surely 'twas another man?'

'It was in the parlour at the public-house; you were almost in the dark.' And John added a few details as to the particular blows, which amounted to proof itself.

'Then I heartily ask your pardon for saying 'twas a lie!' cried Festus, advancing with extended hand and a genial smile. 'Sure, if I had know 'twas you, I wouldn't have insulted you by denying it.'

'That was why you didn't challenge me, then?'

'That was it! I wouldn't for the world have hurt your nice sense of honour by letting ye go unchallenged, if I had known! And now, you see, unfortunately I can't mend the mistake. So long a time has passed since it happened that the heat of my temper is gone off. I couldn't oblige ye, try how I might, for I am not a man, trumpet-major, that can butcher in cold blood—no, not I, nor you neither, from what I know of ye. So, willy-nilly, we must fain let it pass, eh?'

'We must, I suppose,' said John, smiling

grimly. 'Who did you think I was, then, that night when I boxed you all round ?'

'No, don't press me,' replied the yeoman. 'I can't reveal; it would be disgracing myself to show how very wide of the truth the mockery of wine was able to lead my senses. We will let it be buried in eternal mixens of forgetfulness.'

'As you wish,' said the trumpet-major, loftily. 'But if you ever *should* think you knew it was me, why, you know where to find me ?' And Loveday walked away.

The instant that he was gone Festus shook his fist at the evening star, which happened to lie in the same direction as that taken by the dragoon.

'Now for my revenge! Duels? Lifelong disgrace to me if ever I fight with a man of blood below my own! There are other remedies for upper-class souls! . . . Matilda—that's my way.'

Festus strode along till he reached the Hall, where Cripplestraw appeared gazing at him from under the arch of the porter's lodge. Derriman dashed open the entrance-hurdle with such violence that the whole row of them fell flat in the mud.

'Mercy, Maister Festus!' said Cripplestraw. ' " Surely," I says to myself when I see ye a-coming, " surely Maister Festus is fuming like that because there's no chance of the enemy coming this year after all." '

'Cr-r-ripplestraw! I have been wounded to the heart,' replied Derriman, with a lurid brow.

'And the man yet lives, and you wants yer horse-pistols instantly? Certainly, Maister F——.'

'No, Cripplestraw, not my pistols, but my

new-cut clothes, my heavy gold seals, my silver-topped cane, and my buckles that cost more money than he ever saw. Yes, I must tell somebody, and I'll tell you, because there's no other fool near. He loves her heart and soul. He's poor; she's tip-top genteel, and not rich. I am rich, by comparison. I'll court the pretty play-actress, and win her before his eyes.'

' Play-actress, Maister Derriman ?'

'Yes. I saw her this very day, met her by accident, and spoke to her. She's still in Weymouth—perhaps because of him. I can meet her at any hour of the day—— But I don't mean to marry her; not I. I will court her for my pastime, and to annoy him. It will be all the more death to him that I don't want her. Then perhaps he will say to me, 'You have taken my one ewe lamb' —meaning that I am the king, and he's the poor man, as in the church verse ; and he'll beg for mercy when 'tis too late—unless, meanwhile, I shall have tired of my new toy. Saddle the horse, Cripplestraw, to-morrow at ten.'

Full of this resolve to scourge John Loveday to the quick through his passion for Miss Johnson, Festus came out booted and spurred at the time appointed, and set off on his morning ride.

Miss Johnson's theatrical engagement having long ago terminated, she would have left Weymouth with the rest of the visitors had not matrimonial hopes detained her there. These had nothing whatever to do with John Loveday, as may be imagined, but with a stout, staid boat-builder on the Old Quay, who had shown much interest in her impersonations. Unfortunately this substantial man had not been quite so attentive since the end of the season as his previous manner led her to expect; and it was a great pleasure to the lady to see Mr. Derriman leaning over the harbour bridge with his eyes fixed upon her as she came towards it after a stroll past her elderly wooer's house.

'Od take it, ma'am, you didn't tell me when I saw you last that the tooting man with the blue jacket and lace was yours devoted?' began Festus.

'Who do you mean?' In Matilda's ever-changing emotional interests, John Loveday was a stale and unprofitable personality.

'Why, that trumpet-major man.'

'Oh! What of him?'

'Come; he loves you, and you know it, ma'am.'

She knew, at any rate, how to take the

current when it served.    So she glanced
at Festus, folded her lips meaningly, and
nodded.

'I've come to cut him out.'

She shook her head, it being unsafe to
speak till she knew a little more of the subject.

'What!' said Festus, reddening, 'do
you mean to say that you think of him
seriously—you, who might look so much
higher?'

'Constant dropping will wear away a
stone; and you should only hear his plead-
ing! His handsome face is impressive, and
his manners are—oh, so genteel! I am not
rich; I am, in short, a poor lady of decayed
family, who has nothing to boast of but my
blood and ancestors, and they won't find a
body in food and clothing—— I hold the
world but as the world, Derrimanio—a stage

where every man must play a part, and mine
a sad one!' She dropped her eyes thoughtfully and sighed.

'We will talk of this,' said Festus, much
affected. 'Let us walk to the Look-out.'

She made no objection, and said, as they
turned that way, 'Mr. Derriman, a long
time ago I found something belonging to
you; but I have never yet remembered to return it.' And she drew from her bosom the
paper which Anne had dropped in the
meadow when eluding the grasp of Festus
on that summer day.

'Zounds, I smell fresh meat!' cried
Festus when he had looked it over. ''Tis
in my uncle's writing, and 'tis what I heard
him singing on the day the French didn't
come, and afterwards saw him marking in
the road. 'Tis something he's got hid away.

Give me the paper, there's a dear ; 'tis worth sterling gold !'

'Halves, then ?' said Matilda, tenderly.

'Gad, yes — anything !' replied Festus, blazing into a smile, for she had looked up in her best new manner at the possibility that he might be worth the winning.   They went up the steps to the summit of the cliff, and dwindled over it against the sky.

## CHAPTER XXXVII.

### REACTION.

THERE was no letter from Bob, though December had passed, and the new year was two weeks old. His movements were, however, pretty accurately registered in the papers, which John still brought, but which Anne no longer read. During the second week in December the 'Victory' sailed for Sheerness, and on the 9th of the following January the public funeral of Lord Nelson took place in St. Paul's.

Then there came a meagre line addressed to the family in general. Bob's new Portsmouth attachment was not mentioned, but he

told them that he had been one of the eight-
and-forty seamen who walked two-and-two in
the funeral procession, and that Captain
Hardy had borne the banner of emblems on
the same occasion. The crew was soon to
be paid off at Chatham, when he thought of
returning to Portsmouth for a few days to see
a valued friend. After that he should come
home.

But the spring advanced without bringing
him, and John watched Anne Garland's
desolation with augmenting desire to do
something towards consoling her. The old
feelings, so religiously held in check, were
stimulated to rebelliousness, though they did
not show themselves in any direct manner as
yet.

The miller, in the meantime, who seldom
interfered in such matters, was observed to
look meaningly at Anne and the trumpet-

major from day to day; and by-and-by he spoke privately to John.

His words were short and to the point: Anne was very melancholy; she had thought too much of Bob. Now 'twas plain that they had lost him for many years to come. Well; he had always felt that of the two he would rather John married her. Now John might settle down there, and succeed where Bob had failed. 'So if you could get her, my sonny, to think less of him and more of thyself, it would be a good thing for all.'

An inward excitement had risen in John; but he suppressed it and said firmly—

'Fairness to Bob before everything!'

'He hev forgot her, and there's an end on't.'

'She's not forgot him.'

'Well, well; think it over.'

This discourse was the cause of his pen-

ning a letter to his brother.   He begged for
a distinct statement whether, as John at first
supposed, Bob's verbal renunciation of Anne
on the quay had been only a momentary
ebullition of friendship, which it would be
cruel to take literally ; or whether, as seemed
now, it had passed from a hasty resolve to a
standing purpose, persevered in for his own
pleasure, with not a care for the result on poor
Anne.

John waited anxiously for the answer,
but no answer came ; and the silence seemed
even more significant than a letter of assurance could have been of his absolution from
further support to a claim which Bob himself
had so clearly renounced.   Thus it happened
that paternal pressure, brotherly indifference,
and his own released impulse operated in one
delightful direction, and the trumpet-major

once more approached Anne as in the old time.

But it was not till she had been left to herself for a full five months, and the blue-bells and ragged-robins of the following year were again making themselves common to the rambling eye, that he directly addressed her. She was tying up a group of tall flowering plants in the garden : she knew that he was behind her, but she did not turn. She had subsided into a placid dignity which enabled her when watched to perform any little action with seeming composure—very different from the flutter of her inexperienced days.

'Are you never going to turn round ?' he at length asked good-humouredly.

She then did turn, and looked at him for a moment without speaking ; a certain suspicion looming in her eyes, as if suggested by his perceptible want of ease.

'How like summer it is getting to feel, is it not?' she said.

John admitted that it was getting to feel like summer; and, bending his gaze upon her with an earnestness which no longer left any doubt of his subject, went on to ask, 'Have you ever in these last weeks thought of how it used to be between us?'

She replied quickly, 'Oh, John, you shouldn't begin that again. I am almost another woman now!'

'Well, that's all the more reason why I should, isn't it?'

Anne looked thoughtfully to the other end of the garden, faintly shaking her head; 'I don't quite see it like that,' she returned.

'You feel yourself quite free, don't you?'

'*Quite* free!' she said instantly, and with

proud distinctness ; her eyes fell, and she repeated more slowly, 'Quite free.'    Then her
thoughts seemed to fly from herself to him.
' But you are not ? '

   ' I am not ? '

   ' Miss Johnson ! '

   ' Oh—that woman !   You know as well as
I that was all  make up, and that  I never  for
a moment thought of her.'

   ' I  had  an  idea  you  were  acting ; but  I
wasn't sure.'

   ' Well, that's nothing now.    Anne, I want
to relieve  your  life ;  to  cheer  you  in  some
way ; to make some amends for my brother's
bad conduct.    If you cannot love me, liking
will  be  well  enough.    I  have  thought  over
every side of it so many times—for months
have  I  been  thinking  it  over—and  I  am at
last  sure  that  I  do  right  to  put  it  to  you in
this  way.    That  I  don't  wrong  Bob  I  am

quite convinced. As far as he is concerned
we be both free. Had I not been sure of
that I would never have spoken. Father
wants me to take on the mill, and it will
please him if you can give me one little hope ;
it will make the house go on altogether better
if you can think o' me.'

'You are generous and good, John,' she
said, as a big round tear bowled helter-skelter
down her face and hat-strings.

'I am not that ; I fear I am quite the
opposite,' he said, without looking at her.
'It would be all gain to me—— But you
have not answered my question.'

She lifted her eyes. 'John, I cannot!'
she said, with a cheerless smile. 'Posi-
tively I cannot. Will you make me a
promise ?'

'What is it ?'

'I want you to promise first—— Yes, it

is dreadfully unreasonable,' she added, in a mild distress. 'But do promise!'

John by this time seemed to have a feeling that it was all up with him for the present. 'I promise,' he said, listlessly.

'It is that you won't speak to me about this for *ever* so long,' she returned, with emphatic kindliness.

'Very good,' he replied; 'very good. Dear Anne, you don't think I have been unmanly or unfair in starting this anew?'

Anne looked into his face without a smile. 'You have been perfectly natural,' she murmured. 'And so I think have I.'

John, mournfully: 'You will not avoid me for this, or be afraid of me? I will not break my word. I will not worry you any more.'

'Thank you, John. You need not have said worry; it isn't that.'

'Well, I am very blind and stupid. I have been hurting your heart all the time without knowing it. It is my fate I suppose. Men who love women the very best always blunder and give more pain than those who love them less.'

Anne laid one of her hands in the other as she softly replied, looking down at them, 'No one loves me as well as you, John ; nobody in the world is so worthy to be loved ; and yet I cannot anyhow love you rightly.' And lifting her eyes, 'But I do so feel for you that I will try as hard as I can to think about you.'

'Well, that is something,' he said, smiling. 'You say I must not speak about it again for ever so long ; how long ?'

'Now that's not fair,' Anne retorted, going down the garden, and leaving him alone.

About a week passed. Then one afternoon the miller walked up to Anne indoors, a weighty topic being expressed in his tread.

'I was so glad, my honey,' he began, with a knowing smile, 'to see that from the mill-window last week.' He flung a nod in the direction of the garden.

Anne innocently inquired what it could be.

'Jack and you in the garden together,' he continued, laying his hand gently on her shoulder and stroking it. 'It would so please me, my dear little girl, if you could get to like him better than that weathercock, Master Bob.'

Anne shook her head; not in forcible negation, but to imply a kind of neutrality.

'Can't you? Come now,' said the miller.

She threw back her head with a little laugh of grievance. 'How you all beset me!' she expostulated. 'It makes me feel very wicked in not obeying you, and being faithful—faithful to——' But she could not trust that side of the subject to words. 'Why would it please you so much?' she asked.

'John is as steady and staunch a fellow as ever blowed a trumpet. I've always thought you might do better with him than with Bob. Now I've a plan for taking him into the mill, and letting him have a comfortable time o't after his long knocking about; but so much depends upon you that I must bide a bit till I see what your pleasure is about the poor fellow. Mind, my dear, I don't want to force ye; I only just ask ye.'

Anne meditatively regarded the miller from under her shady eyelids, the fingers of one hand playing a silent tattoo on her bosom.

'I don't know what to say to you,' she answered brusquely, and went away.

But these discourses were not without their effect upon the extremely conscientious mind of Anne. They were, moreover, much helped by an incident which took place one evening in the autumn of this year, when John came to tea. Anne was sitting on a low stool in front of the fire, her hands clasped across her knee. John Loveday had just seated himself on a chair close behind her, and Mrs. Loveday was in the act of filling the teapot from the kettle which hung in the chimney exactly above Anne. The kettle slipped forward suddenly; whereupon John jumped from the chair and put his own two hands over Anne's just in time to shield them, and the precious knee she clasped, from the jet of scalding water which had directed itself upon that point. The accidental overflow was instantly checked by Mrs. Loveday ; but what had come was received by the devoted trumpet-major on the backs of his hands.

Anne, who had hardly been aware that he was behind her, started up like a person awakened from a trance. 'What have you done to yourself, poor John, to keep it off me !' she cried, looking at his hands.

John reddened emotionally at her words. ' It is a bit of a scald, that's all,' he replied, drawing a finger across the back of one hand, and bringing off the skin by the touch.

'You are scalded painfully, and I not at all.' She gazed into his kind face as she had never gazed there before, and when Mrs. Loveday came back with oil and other liniments for the wound Anne would let nobody dress it but herself. It seemed as if her coyness had all gone, and when she had done all that lay in her power she still sat by

him.   At his departure she said what she
had never said to him in her life before:
'Come again soon!'

In short, that impulsive act of devotion,
the last of a series of the same tenor, had
been the added drop which finally turned
the wheel. John's character deeply impressed
her.   His determined steadfastness to his
lode-star won her admiration, the more especially as that star was herself.   She began to
wonder more and more how she could have
so persistently held out against his advances
before Bob came home to renew girlish
memories which had by that time got considerably weakened.   Could she not, after all,
please the miller, and try to listen to John?
By so doing she would make a worthy man
happy, the only sacrifice being at worst that
of her unworthy self, whose future was no
longer valuable.   'As for Bob, the woman

is to be pitied who loves him,' she reflected indignantly, and persuaded herself that, whoever the woman might be, she was not Anne Garland.

After this there was something of recklessness and something of pleasantry in the young girl's manner of making herself an example of the triumph of pride and common sense over memory and sentiment. Her attitude had been epitomised in her defiant singing at the time she learnt that Bob was not leal and true. John, as was inevitable, came again almost immediately, drawn thither by the sun of her first smile on him, and the words which had accompanied it. And now instead of going off to her little pursuits up-stairs, down-stairs, across the room, in the corner, or to any place except where he happened to be, as had been her custom hitherto, she remained seated near him, returning interesting answers to his general remarks, and at every opportunity letting him know that at last he had found favour in her eyes.

The day was fine, and they went out of doors, where Anne endeavoured to seat herself on the sloping stone of the window-sill.

'How good you have become lately,' said John, standing over her and smiling in the sunlight which blazed against the wall. 'I fancy you have stayed at home this afternoon on my account.'

'Perhaps I have,' she said, gaily :

'"Do whatever we may for him, dame, we cannot do too
       much,
   For he's one that has guarded our land."

And he has done more that that : he has saved me from a dreadful scalding. The back of your hand will not be well for a long time, John, will it ?'

He held out his hand to regard its condi-
tion, and the next natural thing was to take
hers.  There was a glow upon his face when
he did it : his star was at last on a fair way
towards the zenith after its long and weary
declination.  The least penetrating eye could
have perceived that Anne had resolved to
let him woo, possibly in her temerity to let
him win.  Whatever silent sorrow might be
locked up in her it was by this time thrust
a long way down from the light.

' I want you to go somewhere with me if
you will,' he said, still holding her hand.

' Yes ?  Where is it ? '

He pointed to a distant hill-side which,
hitherto green, had within the last few days
begun to show scratches of white on its face.
' Up there,' he said.

' I see little figures of men moving about.
What are they doing ? '

'Cutting out a huge picture of the king on horseback in the earth of the hill. The king's head is to be as big as our mill-pond and his body as big as this garden; he and the horse will cover more than an acre. When shall we go?'

'Whenever you please,' said she.

'John!' cried Mrs. Loveday from the front door. 'Here's a friend come for you.'

John went round, and found his trusty lieutenant, Trumpeter Buck, waiting for him. A letter had come to the barracks for John in his absence, and the trumpeter, who was going for a walk, had brought it along with him. Buck then entered the mill to discuss, if possible, a mug of last year's mead with the miller; and John proceeded to read his letter, Anne being still round the corner where he had left her. When he had read a few words he turned as pale as a sheet, but he did not move, and perused the writing to the end.

Afterwards he laid his elbow against the wall, and put his palm to his head, thinking with painful intentness. Then he took himself vigorously in hand, as it were, and gradually became natural again. When he parted from Anne to go home with Buck she noticed nothing different in him.

In barracks that evening he read the letter again. It was from Bob; and the agitating contents were these :—

'DEAR JOHN,—I have drifted off from writing till the present time because I have not been clear about my feelings ; but I have discovered them at last, and can say beyond doubt that I mean to be faithful to my dearest Anne after all. The fact is, John,

I've got into a bit of a scrape, and I've a secret to tell you about it (which must go no further on any account). On landing last autumn I fell in with a young woman, and we got rather warm as folks do; in short we liked one another well enough for a while. But I have got into shoal water with her, and have found her to be a terrible take-in. Nothing in her at all—no sense, no niceness, all tantrums and empty noise, John, though she seemed monstrous clever at first. So my heart comes back to its old anchorage. I hope my return to faithfulness will make no difference to you. But as you showed by your looks at our parting that you should not accept my offer to give her up—made in too much haste, as I have since found—I feel that you won't mind that I have returned to the path of honour. I dare not write to Anne as yet, and please do not let her know

a word about the other young woman, or
there will be the devil to pay. I shall come
home and make all things right, please God.
In the meantime I should take it as a kindness,
John, if you would keep a brotherly eye upon
Anne, and guide her mind back to me. I
shall die of sorrow if anybody sets her against
me, for my hopes are getting bound up in
her again quite strong. Hoping you are
jovial, as times go, I am,

'Your affectionate brother,

'ROBERT.'

When the cold daylight fell upon John's
face, as he dressed himself next morning, the
incipient yesterday's wrinkle in his forehead
had become permanently graven there. He
had resolved, for the sake of that only brother
whom he had nursed as a baby, instructed as
a child, and protected and loved always, to

pause in his procedure for the present, and at least do nothing to hinder Bob's restoration to favour, if a genuine, even though temporarily smothered, love for Anne should still hold possession of him. But having arranged to take her to see the excavated figure of the king, he started for Overcombe during the day, as if nothing had occurred to check the smooth course of his love.

## CHAPTER XXXVIII.

### A DELICATE SITUATION.

'I AM ready to go,' said Anne, as soon as he arrived.

He paused as if taken aback by her readiness, and replied with much uncertainty, 'Would it—wouldn't it be better to put it off till there is less sun?'

The very slightest symptom of surprise arose in her as she rejoined, 'But the weather may change; or had we better not go at all?'

'Oh, no!—it was only a thought. We will start at once.'

And along the vale they went, John

keeping himself about a yard from her right hand. When the third field had been crossed they came upon half-a-dozen little boys at play.

'Why don't he clasp her to his side, like a man?' said the biggest and rudest boy.

'Why don't he clasp her to his side, like a man?' echoed all the rude smaller boys in a chorus.

The trumpet-major turned, and, after some running, succeeded in smacking two of them with his switch, returning to Anne breathless. 'I am ashamed they should have insulted you so,' he said, blushing for her.

'They said no harm, poor boys,' she replied, reproachfully.

Poor John was dumb with perception. The gentle hint upon which he would have eagerly spoken only one short day ago was now like fire to his wound.

They presently came to some stepping-stones across a brook. John crossed first without turning his head, and Anne, just lifting the skirt of her dress, crossed behind him. When they had reached the other side a village girl and a young shepherd approached the brink to cross. Anne stopped and watched them. The shepherd took a hand of the young girl in each of his own, and walked backward over the stones, facing her, and keeping her upright by his grasp, both of them laughing as they went.

'What are you staying for, Miss Garland?' asked John.

'I was only thinking how happy they are,' she said, quietly; and withdrawing her eyes from the tender pair, she turned and followed him, not knowing that the seeming sound of a passing bumble-bee was a suppressed groan from John.

When they reached the hill they found forty navvies at work removing the dark sod so as to lay bare the chalk beneath. The equestrian figure that their shovels were forming was scarcely intelligible to John and Anne now they were close, and after pacing from the horse's head down his breast to his hoof, back by way of the king's bridle-arm, past the bridge of his nose, and into his cocked-hat, Anne said that she had had enough of it, and stepped out of the chalk clearing upon the grass. The trumpet-major had remained all the time in a melancholy attitude within the rowel of his Majesty's right spur.

'My shoes are caked with chalk,' she said as they walked downwards again ; and she drew back her dress to look at them. 'How can I get some of it cleared off ?'

'If you was to wipe them in the long grass there,' said John, pointing to a spot where the blades were rank and dense, 'some of it would come off.' Having said this, he walked on with religious firmness.

Anne raked her little feet on the right side, on the left side, over the toe, and behind the heel ; but the tenacious chalk held its own. Panting with her exertion she gave it up, and at length overtook him.

'I hope it is right now ?' he said, looking gingerly over his shoulder.

'No, indeed !' said she. 'I wanted some assistance—some one to steady me. It is so hard to stand on one foot and wipe the other without support. I was in danger of toppling over, and so gave it up.'

'Merciful stars, what an opportunity !' thought the poor fellow while she waited for him to offer help. But his lips remained closed, and she went on with a pouting smile :

'You seem in such a hurry ! Why are you in such a hurry ? After all the fine things you have said about—about caring so much for me, and all that, you won't stop for anything.'

It was too much for John. 'Upon my heart and life my dea—' he began. Here Bob's letter crackled warningly in his waistcoat pocket as he laid his hand asseveratingly upon his breast, and he became suddenly sealed up to dumbness and gloom as before.

When they reached home Anne sank upon a stool outside the door, fatigued with her excursion. Her first act was to try to pull off her shoe—it was a difficult matter ; but John stood beating with his switch the leaves of the creeper on the wall

'Mother—David—Molly, or somebody—do come and help me to pull off these dirty shoes!' she cried aloud at last. 'Nobody helps me in anything!'

'I am very sorry,' said John, coming towards her with incredible slowness and an air of unutterable depression.

'Oh, I can do without *you*. David is best,' she returned, as the old man approached and removed the obnoxious shoes in a trice.

Anne was amazed at this sudden change from devotion to crass indifference. On entering her room she flew to the glass, almost expecting to learn that some extraordinary change had come over her pretty countenance, rendering her intolerable for evermore. But it was, if anything, fresher than usual, on account of the exercise. 'Well!' she said retrospectively. For the first time since their acquaintance she had this week encouraged him ; and for the first time he had shown that encouragement was useless. ' But perhaps he does not clearly understand,' she added, serenely.

When he next came it was, to her surprise, to bring her newspapers, now for some time discontinued. As soon as she saw them she said, ' I do not care for newspapers.'

' The shipping news is very full and long to-day, though the print is rather small.'

' I take no further interest in the shipping news,' she replied with cold dignity.

She was sitting by the window, inside the table, and hence when, in spite of her negations, he deliberately unfolded the paper and began to read about the Royal Navy she could hardly rise and go away. With a stoical mien he read on to the end of the

report, bringing out the name of Bob's ship
with tremendous force.

'No,' she said at last, 'I'll hear no more.
Let me read to you.'

The trumpet-major sat down. Anne
turned to the military news, delivering every
detail with much apparent enthusiasm.
'That's the subject *I* like!' she said, fer-
vently.

'But—but Bob is in the navy now, and
will most likely rise to be an officer. And
then—'

'What is there like the army?' she interrupted. 'There is no smartness about sailors.
They waddle like ducks, and they only fight
stupid battles that no one can form any idea
of. There is no science nor stratagem in
sea fights—nothing more than what you see
when two rams run their heads together in a
field to knock each other down. But in

military battles there is such art, and such
splendour, and the men are so smart, particularly the horse-soldiers. Oh, I shall never
forget what gallant men you all seemed when
you came and pitched your tents on the
downs! I like the cavalry better than anything I know; and the dragoons the best of
the cavalry—and the trumpeters the best of
the dragoons!'

'Oh, if it had but come a little sooner!'
moaned John within him. He replied as
soon as he could regain self-command, ' I am
glad Bob is in the navy at last—he is so much
more fitted for that than the merchant-
service—so brave by nature, ready for any
daring deed. I have heard ever so much
more about his doings on board the " Victory."
Captain Hardy took special notice that when
he——'

'I don't want to know anything more

about it,' said Anne, impatiently ; 'of course
sailors fight ; there's nothimg else to do in a
ship, since you can't run away. You may as
well fight and be killed as be killed not
fighting.'

'Still it is his character to be careless of
himself where the honour of his country is
concerned,' John pleaded. 'If you had only
known him as a boy you would own it. He
would always risk his own life to save anybody else's. Once when a cottage was afire
up the lane he rushed in for a baby, al-
though he was only a boy himself, and he
had the narrowest escape. We have got his
hat now with the hole burnt in it. Shall I
get it and show it to you ?'

'No—I don't wish it. It has nothing to
do with me.' But as he persisted in his
course towards the door, she added, 'Ah !
you are leaving because I am in your way.

You want to be alone while you read the paper—I will go at once.   I did not see that I was interrupting you.'   And she rose as if to retreat.

'No, no!   I would rather be interrupted by *you* than . . . . Oh, Miss Garland, excuse me! I'll just speak to father in the mill, now I am here.'

It is scarcely necessary to state that Anne (whose unquestionable gentility amid somewhat homely surroundings has been many times insisted on in the course of this history) was usually the reverse of a woman with a coming-on disposition; but whether from pique at his manner, or from wilful adherence to a course rashly resolved on, or from coquettish maliciousness in reaction from long depression, or from any other thing,—so it was that she would not let him go.

'Trumpet-major,' she said, recalling him.

'Yes?' he replied timidly.

'The bow of my cap-ribbon has come untied, has it not?' She turned and fixed her bewitching glance upon him.

The bow was just over her forehead, or, more precisely, at the point where the organ of comparison merges in that of benevolence, according to the phrenological theory of Gall. John, thus brought to, endeavoured to look at the bow in a skimming, duck-and-drake fashion, so as to avoid dipping his own glance as far as to the plane of his interrogator's eyes. 'It is untied,' he said, drawing back a little.

She came nearer, and asked, 'Will you tie it for me, please?'

As there was no help for it, he nerved himself and assented. As her head only reached to his fourth button she necessarily

looked up for his convenience, and John
began fumbling at the bow. Try as he
would, it was impossible to touch the ribbon
without getting his finger tips mixed with the
curls of her forehead.

'Your hand shakes—ah! you have been
walking fast,' she said.

'Yes—yes.'

'Have you almost done it?' She inqui-
ringly directed her gaze upward through his
fingers.

'No—not yet,' he faltered in a warm
sweat of emotion, his heart going like a flail.

'Then be quick, please.'

'Yes, I will, Miss Garland! B—B—Bob
is a very good fel——'

'Not that man's name to me!' she interrupted.

John was silent instantly, and nothing was
to be heard but the rustling of the ribbon;

till his hands once more blundered among the curls, and then touched her forehead.

'O, good God!' ejaculated the trumpet-major in a whisper, turning away hastily to the corner-cupboard, and resting his face upon his hand.

'What's the matter, John?' said she.

'I can't do it!'

'What?'

'Tie your cap-ribbon.'

'Why not?'

'Because you are so . . . ! because I am clumsy, and never could tie a bow.'

'You are clumsy indeed,' answered Anne, and went away.

After this she felt injured, for it seemed to show that he rated her happiness as of meaner value than Bob's; since he had persisted in his idea of giving Bob another chance when she had implied that it was her wish to do otherwise. Could Miss Johnson have anything to do with his firmness? An opportunity of testing him in this direction occurred some days later. She had been up the village, and met John at the mill-door.

'Have you heard the news? Matilda Johnson is going to be married to young Derriman.'

Anne stood with her back to the sun, and as he faced her, his features were searchingly exhibited. There was no change whatever in them, unless it were that a certain light of interest kindled by her question turned to complete and blank indifference. 'Well, as times go, it is not a bad match for her,' he said, with a phlegm which was hardly that of a lover.

John on his part was beginning to find these temptations almost more than he could bear. But being quartered so near to his father's house it was unnatural not to visit him, especially when at any moment the regiment might be ordered abroad, and a separation of years ensue ; and as long as he went there he could not help seeing her.

The year changed from green to gold, and from gold to grey, but little change came over the house of Loveday. During the last twelve months Bob had been occasionally heard of as upholding his country's honour in Denmark, the West Indies, Gibraltar, Malta, and other places about the globe, till the family received a short letter stating that he had arrived again at Portsmouth. At Portsmouth Bob seemed disposed to remain, for though sometime elapsed without further intelligence, the gallant seaman never appeared at Overcombe. Then on a sudden John learnt that Bob's long-talked-of promotion for signal services rendered was to

be an accomplished fact. The trumpet-major
at once walked off to Overcombe, and reached
the village in the early afternoon. Not one
of the family was in the house at the moment,
and John strolled onwards over the hill, without much thought of direction till, lifting his
eyes, he beheld Anne Garland coming
towards him with a little basket upon her
arm.

At first John blushed with delight at the
sweet vision ; but, recalled by his conscience,
the blush of delight was at once mangled and
slain. He looked for a means of retreat. But
the field was open, and a soldier was a con-
spicuous object : there was no escaping her.

'It was kind of you to come,' she said,
with an inviting smile.

'It was quite by accident,' he answered,
with an indifferent laugh. 'I thought you
was at home.'

Anne blushed and said nothing, and they rambled on together. In the middle of the field rose a fragment of stone wall in the form of a gable, known as Faringdon Ruin; and when they had reached it John paused and politely asked her if she were not a little tired with walking so far. No particular reply was returned by the young lady, but they both stopped, and Anne seated herself on a stone, which had fallen from the ruin to the ground.

'A church once stood here,' observed John in a matter-of-fact tone.

'Yes, I have often shaped it out in my mind,' she returned. 'Here where I sit must have been the altar.'

'True; this standing bit of wall was the chancel end.'

Anne had been adding up her little studies of the trumpet-major's character, and

was surprised to find how the brightness of
that character increased in her eyes with each
examination.    A kindly and gentle sensation
was again aroused in her.    Here was a
neglected heroic man, who, loving her to distraction, deliberately doomed himself to pen-
sive shade to avoid even the appearance of
standing in a brother's way.

'If the altar stood here, hundreds of
people have been made man and wife just
there, in past times,' she said, with calm
deliberateness, throwing a little stone on a
spot about a yard westward.

John annihilated another tender burst and
replied, ' Yes, this field used to be a village.
My grandfather could call to mind when
there were houses here.    But the squire
pulled 'em down, because poor folk were an
eyesore to him.'

' Do you know, John, what you once

asked me to do ? ' she continued, not accepting the digression, and turning her eyes upon him.

'In what sort of way ? '

'In the matter of my future life, and yours.'

'I am afraid I don't.'

'John Loveday ! '

He turned his back upon her for a moment, that she might not see his face. 'Ah ! —I do remember,' he said at last, in a dry, small, repressed voice.

'Well—need I say more ? Isn't it sufficient ? '

'It would be sufficient,' answered the unhappy man. 'But——'

She looked up with a reproachful smile, and shook her head. 'That summer,' she went on, 'you asked me ten times if you asked me once. I am older now; much more of a woman, you know; and my opinion is changed about some people; especially about one.'

'Oh, Anne, Anne!' he burst out as, racked between honour and desire, he snatched up her hand. The next moment it fell heavily to her lap. He had absolutely relinquished it half-way to his lips.

'I have been thinking lately,' he said, with preternaturally sudden calmness, 'that men of the military profession ought not to —ought to be like St. Paul, I mean.'

'Fie, John; pretending religion!' she said, sternly. 'It isn't that at all. *It's Bob!*'

'Yes!' cried the miserable trumpet-major. 'I have had a letter from him to-day.' He pulled out a sheet of paper from his breast. 'That's it! He's promoted—he's a lieu-tenant, and appointed to a sloop that only cruises on our own coast, so that he'll be at home on leave half his time—he'll be a gentleman some day, and worthy of you !'

He threw the letter into her lap, and drew back to the other side of the gable-wall. Anne jumped up from her seat, flung away the letter without looking at it, and went hastily on. John did not attempt to overtake her. Picking up the letter, he followed in her wake at a distance of a hundred yards.

But, though Anne had withdrawn from his presence thus precipitately, she never thought more highly of him in her life than she did five minutes afterwards, when the excitement of the moment had passed. She saw it all quite clearly ; and his self-sacrifice impressed her so much that the effect was just the reverse of what he had been aiming to produce. The more he pleaded for Bob the more her perverse generosity pleaded for

John. To-day the climax had come—with
what results she had not foreseen.

As soon as the trumpet-major reached the
nearest pen-and-ink he flung himself into a
seat and wrote wildly to Bob :—

'DEAR ROBERT,—I write these few lines
to let you know that if you want Anne Garland you must come at once—you must come
instantly, and post-haste—*or she will be
gone!* Somebody else wants her, and she
wants him! It is your last chance, in the
opinion of—

> 'Your faithful brother and well-wisher,
>
> 'JOHN.

'P.S.—Glad to hear of your promotion
Tell me the day and I'll meet the coach.'

ONE night, about a week later, two men were walking in the dark along the turnpike road towards Overcombe, one of them with a bag in his hand.

'Now,' said the taller of the two, the squareness of whose shoulders signified that he wore epaulettes, 'now you must do the best you can for yourself, Bob. I have done all I can; but th'hast thy work cut out, I can tell thee.'

'I wouldn't have run such a risk for the world,' said the other, in a tone of ingenuous contrition. 'But thou'st see, Jack, I didn't think there was any danger, knowing you was taking care of her, and keeping my place warm for me. I didn't hurry myself, that's true ; but, thinks I, if I get this promotion I am promised I shall naturally have leave, and then I'll go and see 'em all. Gad, I shouldn't have been here now but for your letter !'

'You little think what risks you've run,' said his brother. 'However, try to make up for lost time.'

'All right. And whatever you do, Jack, don't say a word about this other girl. Hang the girl !—I was a great fool, I know ; still, it is over now, and I am come to my senses. I suppose Anne never caught a capful of wind from that quarter ?'

'She knows all about it,' said John, seriously.

'Knows ? By George, then, I'm ruined !'

said Bob, standing stock-still in the road as
if he meant to remain there all night.

'That's what I meant by saying it would
be a hard battle for ye,' returned John, with
the same quietness as before.

Bob sighed and moved on. 'I don't
deserve that woman!' he cried, passionately,
thumping his three upper ribs with his fist.

'I've thought as much myself,' observed
John, with a dryness which was almost bitter.
'But it depends on how thou'st behave in
future.'

'John,' said Bob, taking his brother's
hand, 'I'll be a new man. I solemnly swear
by that eternal milestone staring at me there
that I'll never look at another woman with
the thought of marrying her whilst that
darling is free—no, not if she be a mer-
maiden of light. . . It's a lucky thing that

I'm slipped in on the quarter-deck? it may help me with her—hey?'

'It may with her mother; I don't think it will make much difference with Anne. Still, it is a good thing; and I hope that some day you'll command a big ship.'

Bob shook his head. 'Officers are scarce; but I'm afraid my luck won't carry me so far as that.'

'Did she ever tell you that she mentioned your name to the King?'

The seaman stood still again. 'Never!' he said. 'How did such a thing as that happen, in Heaven's name?'

John described in detail, and they walked on, lost in conjecture.

As soon as they entered the house the re-turned officer of the navy was welcomed with acclamation by his father and David, with mild approval by Mrs. Loveday, and by

Anne not at all—that discreet maiden having carefully retired to her own room some
time earlier in the evening. Bob did not
dare to ask for her in any positive manner;
he just inquired about her health, and that
was all.

'Why, what's the matter with thy face,
my son?' said the miller, staring. 'David,
show a light here.' And a candle was
thrust against Bob's cheek, where there appeared a jagged streak like the geological
remains of a lobster.

'Oh—that's where that rascally French-
man's grenade busted and hit me from the
" Redoubtable," you know, as I told ye in my
letter.'

'Not a word!'

'What, didn't I tell ye? Ah, no; I meant
to, but I forgot it.'

'And here's a sort of dint in yer forehead

too; what do that mean, my dear boy?' said the miller, putting his finger in a chasm in Bob's skull.

'That was done in the Indies. Yes, that was rather a troublesome chop—a cutlass did it. I should have told ye, but I found 'twould make my letter so long that I put it off, and put it off; and at last thought it wasn't worth while.'

John soon rose to take his departure.

'It's all up with me and her, you see,' said Bob to him outside the door. 'She's not even going to see me.'

'Wait a little,' said the trumpet-major.

It was easy enough on the night of the arrival, in the midst of excitement, when blood was warm, for Anne to be resolute in her avoidance of Bob Loveday. But in the morning determination is apt to grow invertebrate; rules of pugnacity are less easily acted up to, and a feeling of live and let live takes possession of the gentle soul. Anne had not meant even to sit down to the same breakfast-table with Bob ; but when the rest were assembled, and had got some way through the substantial repast which was served at this hour in the miller's house, Anne entered. She came silently as a phantom, her eyes cast down, her cheeks pale. It was a good long walk from the door to the table, and Bob made a full inspection of her as she came up to a chair at the remotest corner, in the direct rays of the morning light, where she dumbly sat herself down.

It was altogether different from how she had expected. Here was she, who had done nothing, feeling all the embarrassment ; and Bob, who had done the wrong, feeling apparently quite at ease.

'You'll speak to Bob, won't you, honey?' said the miller after a silence. To meet Bob like this after an absence seemed irregular in his eyes.

'If he wish me to,' she replied, so addressing the miller that no part, scrap, or outlying beam whatever of her glance passed near the subject of her remark.

'He's a lieutenant, you know, dear,' said her mother on the same side; 'and he's been dreadfully wounded.'

'Oh,' said Anne, turning a little towards the false one; at which Bob felt it to be time for him to put in a spoke for himself.

'I am glad to see you,' he said, contritely; 'and how do you do?'

'Very well, thank you.'

He extended his hand. She allowed him to take hers, but only to the extent of a niggardly inch or so. At the same moment she glanced up at him, when their eyes met, and hers were again withdrawn.

The hitch between the two younger members of the household tended to make the breakfast a dull one. Bob was so depressed by her unforgiving manner that he could not throw that sparkle into his stories which their substance naturally required; and when the meal was over, and they went about their different businesses, the pair resembled the two Dromios in seldom or never being, thanks to Anne's subtle contrivances, both in the same room at the same time.

This kind of performance repeated itself during several days. At last, after dogging her hither and thither, leaning with a wrinkled forehead against doorposts, taking an oblique view into the room where she happened to be, picking up worsted balls and getting no thanks, placing a splinter from the ‘Victory,’

several bullets from the ' Redoubtable,' a strip
of the flag, and other interesting relics, carefully labelled, upon her table, and hearing no
more about them than if they had been
pebbles from the nearest brook, he hit upon
a new plan. To avoid him she frequently
sat up-stairs in a window overlooking the
garden. Lieutenant Loveday carefully
dressed himself in a new uniform, which he
had caused to be sent some days before, to
dazzle admiring friends, but which he had
never as yet put on in public or mentioned
to a soul. When arrayed he entered the
sunny garden, and there walked slowly up
and down as he had seen Nelson and Captain
Hardy do on the quarter-deck; but keeping
his right shoulder, on which his one epaulette
was fixed, as much towards Anne's window
as possible.

But she made no sign, though there was

not the least question that she saw him. At the end of half an hour he went in, took off his clothes, and gave himself up to doubt, and the best tobacco.

He repeated the programme on the next afternoon, and on the next, never saying a word within doors about his doings or his notice.

Meanwhile the results in Anne's chamber were not uninteresting. She had been looking out on the first day, and was duly amazed to see a naval officer in full uniform promenading in the path. Finding it to be Bob she left the window with a sense that the scene was not for her; then, from mere curiosity, peeped out from behind the curtain. Well, he was a pretty spectacle, she admitted, relieved as his figure was by a dense mass of sunny, close-trimmed hedge, over which nasturtiums climbed in wild luxu-

riance; and if she could care for him one
bit, which she couldn't, his form would
have been a delightful study, surpassing in
interest even its splendour on the memorable
day of their visit to the Weymouth theatre.
She called her mother; Mrs. Loveday came
promptly.

'Oh, it is nothing,' said Anne, indiffer-
ently; 'only that Bob has got his uniform.'

Mrs. Loveday peeped out, and raised her
hands with delight. 'And he has not said
a word to us about it! What a lovely
epaulette! I must call his father.'

'No, indeed. As I take no interest in
him I shall not let people come into my room
to admire him.'

'Well, you called me,' said her mother.

'It was because I thought you liked fine
clothes. It is what I don't care for.'

Notwithstanding this assertion she again

looked out at Bob the next afternoon when
his footsteps rustled on the gravel, and studied
his appearance under all the varying angles
of the sunlight as if fine clothes and uniforms
were not altogether a matter of indifference.
He certainly was a splendid, gentlemanly,
and gallant sailor from end to end of him;
but then, what were a dashing presentment,
a naval rank, and telling scars, if a man was
fickle-hearted?    However, she peeped on
till the fourth day, and then she did not
peep.   The window was open, she looked
right out, and Bob knew that he had got a
rise to his bait at last.   He touched his hat
to her, keeping his right shoulder forwards,
and said, 'Good day, Miss Garland,' with a
smile.

Anne replied, 'Good day,' with funereal
seriousness; and the acquaintance thus revived led to the interchange of a few words

at supper-time, at which Mrs. Loveday
nodded with satisfaction. But Anne took
especial care that he should never meet her
alone, and to insure this her ingenuity was
in constant exercise. There were so many
nooks and windings on the miller's rambling
premises that she could never be sure he
would not turn up within a foot of her, particularly as his thin shoes were almost noise-
less.

One fine afternoon she accompanied
Molly in search of elder berries for making
the family wine which was drunk by Mrs.
Loveday, Anne, and anybody who could not
stand the rougher and stronger liquors pro-
vided by the miller. After walking rather a
long distance over the down they came to a
grassy hollow, where elder bushes in knots
of twos and threes rose from an uneven bank
and hung their heads towards the south,

black and heavy with bunches of fruit. The charm of fruit-gathering to girls is enhanced in the case of elder berries by the inoffensive softness of the leaves, boughs, and bark, which makes getting into them easy and pleasant to the most indifferent climbers. Anne and Molly had soon gathered a basket-ful, and sending the servant home with it Anne remained in the bush picking and throwing down bunch by bunch upon the grass. She was so absorbed in her occupation of pulling the twigs towards her, and the rustling of their leaves so filled her ears, that it was a great surprise when, on turning her head, she perceived a similar movement to her own among the boughs of the adjoining bush.

At first she thought they were disturbed by being partly in contact with the boughs of her bush; but in a moment Robert

Loveday's face peered from them, at a distance of about a yard from her own. Anne
uttered a little indignant 'Well!' recovered
herself, and went on plucking. Bob thereupon went on plucking likewise.

'I am picking elder berries for your
mother,' said the lieutenant at last, humbly.

'So I see.'

'And I happen to have come to the next
bush to yours.'

'So I see ; but not the reason why.'

Anne was now in the westernmost branches of the bush, and Bob had leant across
into the eastern branches of his. In gather-
ing he swayed towards her, back again, forward again.

'I beg pardon,' he said, when a farther
swing than usual had taken him almost in
contact with her.

'Then why do you do it ?'

'The wind rocks the bough, and the bough rocks me.' She expressed by a look her opinion of this statement in the face of the gentlest breeze ; and Bob pursued : 'I am afraid the berries will stain your pretty hands.'

'I wear gloves.'

'Ah, that's a plan I should never have thought of. Can I help you ?'

'Not at all.'

'You are offended : that's what that means.'

'No,' she said.

'Then will you shake hands ?'

Anne hesitated ; then slowly stretched out her hand, which he took at once. 'That will do,' she said, finding that he did not relinquish it immediately. But as he still held it, she pulled, the effect of which was to draw Bob's swaying person, bough and all, towards her, and herself towards him.

'I am afraid to let go your hand,' said that officer; 'for if I do your spar will fly back, and you will be thrown upon the deck with great violence.'

'I wish you to let me go!'

He accordingly did, and she flew back, but did not by any means fall.

'It reminds me of the times when I used to be aloft clinging to a yard not much bigger than this tree-stem, in the mid-Atlantic, and thinking about you. I could see you in my fancy as plain as I see you now.'

'Me, or some other woman,' retorted Anne, haughtily.

'No!' declared Bob, shaking the bush for emphasis. 'I'll protest that I did not think of anybody but you all the time we were dropping down channel, all the time we

were off Cadiz, all the time through battles
and bombardments.    I seemed to see you in
the smoke, and, thinks I, if I go to Davy's
locker, what will she do ?'

'You didn't think that when you landed
after Trafalgar.'

'Well, now,' said the Lieutenant in
a reasoning tone ; 'that was a curious thing.
You'll hardly believe it, maybe ; but when a
man is away from the woman he loves best
in the port—world, I mean—he can have a
sort of temporary feeling for another without disturbing the old one, which flows along
under the same as ever.'

'I can't believe it, and won't,' said Anne,
firmly.

Molly now appeared with the empty
basket, and when it had been filled from the
heap on the grass, Anne went home with her,
bidding Loveday a frigid adieu.

The same evening, when Bob was absent, the miller proposed that they should all three go to an upper window of the house, to get a distant view of some rockets and illuminations which were to be exhibited in Weymouth at that hour in honour of the King, who had returned this year as usual. They accordingly went up-stairs to an empty attic, placed chairs against the window, and put out the light, Anne sitting in the middle, her mother close by, and the miller behind, smoking. No sign of any pyrotechnic display was visible over Weymouth as yet, and Mrs. Loveday passed the time by talking to the miller, who replied in monosyllables. While this was going on Anne fancied that she heard some one approach, and presently felt sure that Bob was drawing near her in the surrounding darkness; but as the other two had noticed nothing she said not a word.

All at once the swarthy expanse of southward sky was broken by the blaze of several
rockets simultaneously ascending from different ships in the Roads. At the very same
moment a warm mysterious hand slipped
round her own, and gave it a gentle squeeze.

'Oh, dear!' said Anne, with a sudden
start away.

'How nervous you are, child, to be
startled by fireworks so far off,' said Mrs.
Loveday.

'I never saw rockets before,' murmured
Anne, recovering from her surprise.

Mrs. Loveday presently spoke again. 'I
wonder what has become of Bob?'

Anne did not reply, being much exer-
cised in trying to get her hand away from
the one that imprisoned it; and whatever
the miller thought he kept to himself, because
it disturbed his smoking to speak.

Another batch of rockets went up. 'Oh, I never!' said Anne, in a half-suppressed tone, springing in her chair. A second hand had with the rise of the rockets leapt round her waist.

'Poor girl, you certainly must have change of scene at this rate;' said Mrs. Loveday.

'I suppose I must,' murmured the dutiful daughter.

For some minutes nothing further occurred to disturb Anne's serenity. Then a slow, quiet 'a-hem' came from the obscurity of the apartment.

'What, Bob? How long have you been there?' inquired Mrs. Loveday.

'Not long,' said the lieutenant coolly. 'I heard you were all here, and crept up quietly, not to disturb ye.'

'Why don't you wear heels to your shoes

like Christian people, and not creep about so like a cat?'

'Well, it keeps your floors clean to go slip-shod.'

'That's true.'

Meanwhile Anne was gently but firmly trying to pull Bob's arm from her waist, her distressful difficulty being that in freeing her waist she enslaved her hand, and in getting her hand free she enslaved her waist. Finding the struggle a futile one, owing to the invisibility of her antagonist, and her wish to keep its nature secret from the other two, she arose, and saying that she did not care to see any more, felt her way down-stairs. Bob followed, leaving Loveday and his wife to themselves.

'Dear Anne,' he began, when he had got down, and saw her in the candlelight of the large room. But she adroitly passed out at

the other door, at which he took a candle
and followed her to the small room. 'Dear
Anne, do let me speak,' he repeated, as soon
as the rays revealed her figure. But she
passed into the bakehouse before he could
say more; whereupon he perseveringly did
the same. Looking round for her here he
perceived her at the end of the room, where
there were no means of exit whatever.

'Dear Anne,' he began again, setting
down the candle, 'you must try to forgive
me; really you must. I love you the best of
anybody in the wide, wide world. Try to
forgive me; come !' And he imploringly
took her hand.

Anne's bosom began to surge and fall like
a small tide, her eyes remaining fixed upon
the floor; till, when Loveday ventured to
draw her slightly towards him, she burst out
crying. 'I don't like you Bob; I don't !'

she suddenly exclaimed between her sobs.
'I did once, but I don't now—I can't, I
can't; you have been very cruel to me!'
She violently turned away, weeping.

'I have, I have been terribly bad, I
know,' answered Bob, conscience-stricken by
her grief. 'But—if you could only forgive
me—I promise that I'll never do anything
to grieve ye again. Do you forgive me,
Anne?'

Anne's only reply was crying and shaking
her head.

'Let's make it up. Come, say we have
made it up, dear.'

She withdrew her hand, and still keeping
her eyes buried in her handkerchief, said,
'No.'

'Very well, then!' exclaimed Bob, with
sudden determination. 'Now I know my
doom! And whatever you hear of as hap-

pening to me, mind this, you cruel girl, that
it is all your causing!' Saying this he
strode with a hasty tread across the room
into the passage and out at the door, slam-
ming it loudly behind him.

Anne suddenly looked up from her handkerchief, and stared with round wet eyes and
parted lips at the door by which he had
gone. Having remained with suspended
breath in this attitude for a few seconds she
turned round, bent her head upon the table,
and burst out weeping anew with thrice the
violence of the former time. It really
seemed now as if her grief would overwhelm
her, all the emotions which had been suppressed, bottled up, and concealed since
Bob's return having made themselves a sluice
at last.

But such things have their end; and left
to herself in the large, vacant, old apartment,

she grew quieter, and at last calm. At length she took the candle and ascended to her bedroom, where she bathed her eyes and looked in the glass to see if she had made herself a dreadful object. It was not so bad as she had expected, and she went downstairs again.

Nobody was there, and, sitting down, she wondered what Bob had really meant by his words. It was too dreadful to think that he intended to go straight away to sea without seeing her again, and frightened at what she had done, she waited anxiously for his return.

# CHAPTER XL.

## A CALL ON BUSINESS.

HER suspense was interrupted by a very gentle tapping at the door, and then the rustle of a hand over its surface, as if searching for the latch in the dark. The door opened a few inches, and the alabaster face of Uncle Benjy appeared in the slit.

'Oh. Squire Derriman, you frighten me!'

'All alone?' he asked in a whisper.

'My mother and Mr. Loveday are somewhere about the house.'

'That will do,' he said, coming forward. 'I be wherrited out of my life, and I have thought of you again—you yourself, dear

Anne, and not the miller. If you will only take this and lock it up for a few days till I can find another good place for it—if you only would!' And he breathlessly deposited the tin box on the table.

'What, obliged to dig it up from the cellar?'

'Ay; my nephew hath a scent of the place—how, I don't know! but he and a young woman he's met with are searching everywhere. I worked like a wire-drawer to get it up and away while they were scraping in the next cellar. Now where could ye put it, dear? 'Tis only a few documents, and my will, and such like, you know. Poor soul o' me, I'm worn out with running and fright!'

'I'll put it here till I can think of a better place,' said Anne, lifting the box. 'Dear me, how heavy it is!'

'Yes, yes,' said Uncle Benjy, hastily; 'the box is iron, you see. However, take care of it, because I am going to make it worth your while. Ah, you are a good girl, Anne. I wish you was mine!'

Anne looked at Uncle Benjy. She had known for some time that she possessed all the affection he had to bestow.

'Why do you wish that?' she said, simply.

'Now don't ye argue with me. Where d'ye put the coffer?'

'Here,' said Anne, going to the window-seat, which rose as a flap, disclosing a boxed receptacle beneath, as in many old houses.

''Tis very well for the present,' he said, dubiously, and they dropped the coffer in, Anne locking down the seat, and giving him the key. 'Now I don't want ye to be on my side for nothing,' he went on. 'I never did

now, did I ? This is for you.' He handed
her a little packet of paper, which Anne
turned over and looked at curiously. 'I
always meant to do it,' continued Uncle
Benjy, gazing at the packet as it lay in her
hand, and sighing. 'Come, open it, my
dear ; I always meant to do it.'

She opened it and found twenty new
guineas snugly packed within.

'Yes, they are for you. I always meant
to do it !' he said, sighing again.

'But you owe me nothing !' returned
Anne, holding them out.

'Don't say it !' cried Uncle Benjy, cover-
ing his eyes. 'Put 'em away. . . . Well, if
you *don't* want 'em——But put 'em away,
dear Anne ; they are for you, because you
have kept my counsel. Good night t' ye.
Yes, they are for you.'

He went a few steps, and turning back

added anxiously, 'You won't spend 'em in clothes, or waste 'em in fairings, or ornaments of any kind, my dear girl ?'

'I will not,' said Anne. 'I wish you would have them.'

'No, no,' said Uncle Benjy, rushing off to escape their shine. But he had got no farther than the passage when he returned again.

'And you won't lend 'em to anybody, or put 'em into the bank—for no bank is safe in these troublous times. . . . If I was you I'd keep them *exactly* as they be, and not spend 'em on any account. Shall I lock them into my box for ye ?'

'Certainly,' said she ; and the farmer rapidly unlocked the window-bench, opened the box, and locked them in.

''Tis much the best plan,' he said with great satisfaction as he returned the keys to his pocket. 'There they will always be safe, you see, and you won't be exposed to temptation.'

When the old man had been gone a few minutes, the miller and his wife came in, quite unconscious of all that had passed. Anne's anxiety about Bob was again uppermost now, and she spoke but meagrely of old Derriman's visit, and nothing of what he had left. She would fain have asked them if they knew where Bob was, but that she did not wish to inform them of the rupture. She was forced to admit to herself that she had somewhat tried his patience, and that impulsive men had been known to do dark things with themselves at such times.

They sat down to supper, the clock ticked rapidly on, and at length the miller said, 'Bob is later than usual. Where can he be?'

As they both looked at her, she could no longer keep the secret.

'It is my fault,' she cried; 'I have driven him away! What shall I do?'

The nature of the quarrel was at once guessed, and her two elders said no more. Anne rose and went to the front door, where she listened for every sound with a palpitating heart. Then she went in; then she went out: and on one occasion she heard the miller say, 'I wonder what hath passed between Bob and Anne. I hope the chap will come home.'

Just about this time light footsteps were heard without, and Bob bounced into the passage. Anne, who stood back in the dark while he passed, followed him into the room, where her mother and the miller were on the point of retiring to bed, candle in hand.

'I have kept ye up, I fear,' began Bob

cheerily, and apparently without the faintest recollection of his tragic exit from the house. 'But the truth on 't is, I met with Fess Derriman at the ' Duke of York' as I went from here, and there we have been playing Put ever since, not noticing how the time was going. I haven't had a good chat with the fellow for years and years, and really he is an out and out good comrade—a regular hearty! Poor fellow, he's been very badly used. I never heard the rights of the story till now; but it seems that old uncle of his treats him shamefully. He has been hiding away his money so that poor Fess might not have a farthing, till at last the young man has turned, like any other worm, and is now determined to ferret out what he has done with it. The poor young chap hadn't a farthing of ready money till I lent him a couple of guineas—a thing I never did more

willingly in my life.    But the man was very
honourable.    'No; no,' says he, 'don't let
me deprive ye.'    He's going to marry, and
what may you think he is going to do it
for?'

'For love, I hope,' said Anne's mother.

'For money, I suppose, since he's so
short,' said the miller.

'No,' said Bob, 'for *spite*.   He has been
badly served—deuced badly served—by a
woman.    I never heard of a more heartless
case in my life.    The poor chap wouldn't
mention names, but it seems this young
woman has trifled with him in all manner of
cruel ways—pushed him into the river, tried
to steal his horse when he was called out to
defend his country—in short, served him
rascally.    So I gave him the two guineas and
said, "Now let's drink to the hussy's down-
fall!"'

'Oh!' said Anne, having approached behind him.

Bob turned and saw her, and at the same moment Mr. and Mrs. Loveday discreetly retired by the other door.

'Is it peace?' he asked, tenderly.

'Oh yes,' she anxiously replied. 'I—didn't mean to make you think I had no heart.' At this Bob inclined his countenance towards hers. 'No,' she said, smiling through two incipient tears as she drew back. 'You are to show good behaviour for six months, and you must promise not to frighten me again by running off when I—show you how badly you have served me.'

'I am yours obedient—in anything,' cried Bob. 'But am I pardoned?'

Youth is foolish; and does a woman often let her reasoning in favour of the worthier stand in the way of her perverse desire for the less worthy at such times as these? She murmured some soft words, ending with ' Do you repent?'

It would be superfluous to transcribe Bob's answer.

Footsteps were heard without.

' O, begad ; I forgot!' said Bob. ' He's waiting out there for a light.'

' Who ?'

' My friend Derriman.'

' But, Bob, I have to explain.'

But Festus had by this time entered the lobby, and Anne, with a hasty ' Get rid of him at once !' vanished up-stairs.

Here she waited and waited, but Festus did not seem inclined to depart ; and at last, foreboding some collision of interests from Bob's new friendship for this man, she crept into a storeroom which was over the apartment into which Loveday and Festus had gone. By looking through a knot-hole in the floor it was easy to command a view of the room beneath, this being unceiled, with moulded beams and rafters.

Festus had sat down on the hollow window-bench, and was continuing the statement of his wrongs. 'If he only knew what he was sitting upon,' she thought apprehensively, 'how easily he could tear up the flap, lock and all, with his strong arm, and seize upon poor Uncle Benjy's possessions! But he did not appear to know, unless he were acting, which was just possible. After a while he rose, and going to the table lifted the candle to light his pipe. At the moment when the flame began diving into the bowl the door noiselessly opened and a figure slipped across the room to the window-bench, hastily unlocked it, withdrew the box, and beat a retreat. Anne in a moment recognised the

ghostly intruder as Festus Derriman's uncle.
Before he could get out of the room Festus
set down the candle and turned.

'What—Uncle Benjy—haw, haw!  Here
at this time of night?'

Uncle Benjy's eyes grew paralysed, and
his mouth opened and shut like a frog's in a
drought, the action producing no sound.

'What have we got here—a tin box—
the box of boxes?  Why, I'll carry it for
ye, uncle!  I am going home.'

'N—no—no, thanky, Festus : it is n—n—
not heavy at all, thanky,' gasped the squi-
reen.

'Oh, but I must,' said Festus, pulling at
the box.

'Don't let him have it, Bob!' screamed
the excited Anne through the hole in the
floor.

'No, don't let him!' cried the uncle.  ''Tis

a plot—there's a woman at the window waiting to help him!'

Anne's eyes flew to the window, and she
saw Matilda's face pressed against the pane.

Bob, though he did not know whence
Anne's command proceeded, obeyed with
alacrity, pulled the box from the two rela-
tives, and placed it on the table beside him.

'Now, look here, hearties; what's the
meaning o' this?' he said.

'He's trying to rob me of all I possess!'
cried the old man. 'My heart strings seem
as if they were going crack, crack, crack!'

At this instant the miller in his shirt
sleeves entered the room, having got thus
far in his undressing when he heard the noise.
Bob and Festus turned to him to explain;
and when the latter had had his say Bob
added, 'Well, all I know is that this box'—
here he stretched out his hand to lay it upon

the lid for emphasis.  But as nothing but thin air met his fingers where the box had been, he turned, and found that the box was gone, Uncle Benjy having vanished also.

Festus, with an imprecation, hastened to the door, but though the night was not dark Farmer Derriman and his burden were nowhere to be seen.  On the bridge Festus joined a shadowy female form, and they went along the road together, followed for some distance by Bob, lest they should meet with and harm the old man.  But the precaution was unnecessary : nowhere on the road was there any sign of Farmer Derriman, or of the box that belonged to him.  When Bob reentered the house Anne and Mrs. Loveday had joined the miller down-stairs, and then for the first time he learnt who had been the heroine of Festus's lamentable story, with many other particulars of that yeoman's

history which he had never before known.
Bob swore that he would not speak to the
traitor again, and the family retired.

The escape of old Mr. Derriman from
the annoyances of his nephew not only held
good for that night, but for next day, and for
ever. Just after dawn on the following
morning a labouring man, who was going to
his work, saw the old farmer and landowner
leaning over a rail in a mead near his house,
apparently engaged in contemplating the
water of a brook before him. Drawing near
the man spoke, but Uncle Benjy did not
reply. His head was hanging strangely, his
body being supported in its erect position
entirely by the rail that passed under each
arm. On after examination it was found
that Uncle Benjy's poor withered heart had
cracked and stopped its beating from damages
inflicted on it by the excitements of his life,

and of the previous night in particular. The unconscious carcase was little more than a light empty husk, dry and fleshless as that of a dead heron found on a moor in January.

But the tin box was not discovered with or near him. It was searched for all the week, and all the month. The mill-pond was dragged, quarries were examined, woods were threaded, rewards were offered ; but in vain.

At length one day in the spring, when the mill-house was about to be cleaned throughout, the chimney-board of Anne's bedroom, concealing a yawning fire-place, had to be taken down. In the chasm behind it stood the missing deed-box of Farmer Derriman.

Many were the conjectures as to how it had got there. Then Anne remembered that on going to bed on the night of the collision between Festus and his uncle in the room below, she had seen mud on the carpet of her room, and the miller remembered that he had seen foot-prints on the back staircase. The solution of the mystery seemed to be that the late Uncle Benjy, instead of running off from the house with his box, had doubled on getting out of the front door, entered at the back, deposited his box in Anne's chamber where it was found, and then leisurely pursued his way home at the heels of Festus, intending to tell Anne of his trick the next day—an intention that was for ever frustrated by the stroke of death.

Mr. Derriman's solicitor was a Weymouth man, and Anne placed the box in his hands. Uncle Benjy's will was discovered within; and by this testament Anne's queer old friend appointed her sole executrix of his said will, and, more than that, gave and bequeathed to the same young lady all his real and personal estate, with the solitary exception of five small freehold houses in a back street in Weymouth, which were devised to his nephew, Festus, as a sufficient property to maintain him decently, without affording any margin for extravagances. Overcombe Hall, with its muddy quadrangle, archways, mullioned windows, cracked battlements, and weed-grown garden, passed with the rest into the hands of Anne.

# CHAPTER XLI.

### THE SOLDIER'S TEAR.

DURING this exciting time John Loveday seldom or never appeared at the mill. With the recall of Bob, in which he had been sole agent, his mission seemed to be complete.

One mid-day, before Anne had made any change in her manner of living on account of her unexpected acquisistions, Lieutenant Bob came in rather suddenly. He had been to Weymouth, and announced to the arrested senses of the family that the ——th Dragoons were ordered to join Sir Arthur Wellesley in the Peninsula.

These tidings produced a great impression

in the household. John had been so long in the neighbourhood, either at camp or in barracks, that they had almost forgotten the possibility of his being sent away; and they now began to reflect upon the singular infrequency of his calls since his brother's return. There was not much time, however, for reflection, if they wished to make the most of John's farewell visit, which was to be paid the same evening, the departure of the regiment being fixed for next day. A hurried valedictory supper was prepared during the afternoon, and shortly afterwards John arrived.

He seemed to be more thoughtful and a trifle paler than of old, but beyond these traces, which might have been due to the natural wear and tear of time, he showed no signs of gloom. On his way through the town that morning a curious little incident had occurred to him. He was walking past one of the Weymouth churches when a wedding party came forth, the bride and bridegroom being Matilda and Festus Derriman. At sight of the trumpet-major the yeoman had glared triumphantly; Matilda, on her part, had winked at him slily, as much as to say——. But what she meant heaven knows; the trumpet-major did not trouble himself to think, and passed on without returning the mark of confidence with which she had favoured him.

Soon after John's arrival at the mill several of his friends dropped in for the same purpose of bidding adieu. They were mostly the men who had been entertained there on the occasion of the regiment's advent on the down, when Anne and her mother were coaxed in to grace the party by their superior presence; and their well-trained, gallant

manners were such as to make them interesting visitors now as at all times. For it was
a period when romance had not so greatly
faded out of military life as it has done in
these days of short service, heterogeneous
mixing, and transient campaigns; when the
*esprit de corps* was strong, and long expe-
rience stamped noteworthy professional cha-
racteristics even on rank and file : while the
miller's visitors had the additional advantage
of being picked men.

They could not stay so long to-night as
on that earlier and more cheerful occasion,
and the final adieus were spoken at an early
hour. It was no mere playing at departure,
as when they had gone to Exeter barracks,
and there was a warm and prolonged shaking
of hands all round.

'You'll wish the poor fellows good-bye?'
said Bob to Anne, who had not come for-

ward for that purpose like the rest. 'They are going away, and would like to have your good word.'

She then shyly advanced, and every man felt that he must make some pretty speech as he shook her by the hand.

'Good-bye! May you remember us as long as it makes ye happy, and forget us as soon as it makes ye sad,' said Sergeant Brett.

'Good-night! Health, wealth, and long life to ye!' said Sergeant-major Wills, taking her hand from Brett.

'I trust to meet ye again as the wife of a worthy man,' said Trumpeter Buck.

'We'll drink your health throughout the campaign, and so good-bye t' ye,' said Saddler-Sergeant Jones, raising her hand to his lips.

Three others followed with similar re-marks, to each of which Anne blushingly replied as well as she could, wishing them a prosperous voyage, easy conquest, and a speedy return.

But, alas, for that! Battles and skirmishes, advances and retreats, fevers and fatigues, told hard on Anne's gallant friends in the coming time. Of the seven upon whom these wishes were bestowed, five, including the trumpet-major, were dead men within the few following years, and their bones left to moulder in the land of their campaigns.

John lingered behind. When the others were outside, expressing a final farewell to his father, Bob, and Mrs. Loveday, he came to Anne, who remained within.

'But I thought you were going to look in again before leaving?' she said, gently.

'No; I find I cannot. Good-bye!'

'John,' said Anne, holding his right hand in both hers, 'I must tell you something.

You were wise in not taking me at my word
that day. I was greatly mistaken about myself. Gratitude is not love, though I wanted
to make it so for the time. You don't call
me thoughtless for what I did?'

'My dear Anne,' cried John, with more
gaiety than truthfulness, 'don't let yourself
be troubled! What happens is for the best.
Soldiers love here to-day and there to-morrow. Who knows that you won't hear of my
attentions to some Spanish maid before a
month is gone by? 'Tis the way of us, you
know; a soldier's heart is not worth a week's
purchase—ha, ha! Good-bye, good-bye!'

Anne felt the expediency of his manner,
received the affectation as real, and smiled
her reply, not knowing that the adieu was for
evermore, and that John would like a soldier
fall. Then with a tear in his eye he went
out of the door, where he bade farewell to the

miller, Mrs. Loveday, and Bob, who said at parting, 'It's all right, Jack, my dear fellow. After a coaxing that would have been enough to win three ordinary Englishwomen, five French, and ten Mulotters, she has to-day agreed to bestow her hand upon me at the end of six months. Good-bye, Jack, good-bye!'

The candle held by his father shed its waving light upon John's face and uniform as he turned with a farewell smile on the doorstone, backed by the black night ; and in another moment he had plunged into the darkness, the ring of his smart step dying away upon the bridge as he joined his wait-ing companions-in-arms, and went off to blow his trumpet till silenced for ever upon one of the bloody battle-fields of Spain.

THE END.

Spottiswoode & Co., Printers, New-street Square, London.

www.ingramcontent.com/pod-product-compliance
Lightning Source LLC
Chambersburg PA
CBHW020357030726
47496CB00007B/2177